The Mark of the Beast

Charles Owen

Telling Tales: Vol 2

Books by Charles Owen

Novellas:

FIAMMA

CRY CASSANDRA !

Telling Tales:

Vol 1: A CRACK IN THE GLASS

Vol 2: THE MARK OF THE BEAST

Vol 3: MAN OVERBOARD

Vol 4: ESCAPADE

Copyright

CONTENTS

The Mark of the Beast

'I hope I haven't missed anything,' said Virginia, surveying the contents of the open suitcase.

'You never miss anything,' her husband replied.

This was perfectly true. Virginia Loveridge had a meticulous eye for detail and handled every aspect of their lives with almost obsessive efficiency. Everything that Colin could possibly need for a short business trip to Paris had been laid out on the bed for inspection. He watched while each article was lovingly patted into place: the shoes shining like glossy racehorses coaxed into their blue flannel bag: the shirts and ties wrapped in layer upon layer of tissue paper: the sponge bag with its small portmanteau of treasures, each snug in its own waterproof pocket, every item occupying a position in relation to its neighbour hallowed by years of trial and demonstrably no error – a model for any wife so intrepid as to abandon her husband to the vagaries of a commercial hotel on the Rive Gauche for a few days. Finally the lid was closed upon this miracle of foresight and planning and the suitcase placed downstairs just inside the front door to await Colin's departure the following morning.

'It's almost time for your shower, Colin,' Virginia called up to him. 'After that I must make up my diary.'

Annually, on New Year's Day, every event that seemed likely to touch their lives in the following twelve months was entered in Virginia's diary. On the first Sunday in April and September they always drove to Eastbourne to spend the day with Virginia's widowed mother. Equally, the last weekend in June was kept free, for that was when Colin's parents came over from Dartford. Last year the weather had been glorious and they had packed a picnic and spent the afternoon at Northdown Animal Kingdom, which was little more than a ten-minute drive from the house.

The first fortnight in August was no less sacrosanct for it was then that Colin and Virginia took their annual holiday. Virginia would go to a drawer in her desk and find her holiday list and the little Fiat would be packed with everything that they would need, in accordance with a tried and trusted formula. Come rain or shine, on the first of August they would set off for Twin Pines, a comfortable, unpretentious guest house on the Kent coast.

Other entries in the diary were more commonplace, the dates when the boiler and the dishwasher were due for servicing or when the couple should visit the dentist for their annual check-up. The month when it was Virginia's turn to do the church flowers. The weekend when they must drive over to the garden centre and buy the spring bulbs, whose selection had been the subject of earnest debate and careful study of catalogues during many a winter evening. Everything which played its part in the smooth running of that well-ordered household was included. On Sunday evenings, Virginia sat down at the pine desk in the corner of the sitting room. Not until she had finished her work would she reward herself with a look through the window at the tiny front garden with its brick-paved path, neat borders and little patch of well-kept lawn.

Virginia totalled the household expenditure for the week, calculated Colin's average weight for the same period and wrote both figures in the diary in her bold, rather childish hand. Before turning the page to the following week, she would place a modest asterisk in the special section allocated to Saturday evening, confirmation that she and Colin had made love that night. Unfailingly, this agreeable activity took place every Saturday night and varied as little in its performance. When the supper things had been cleared away and the washing-up had been done, they would sit together on the sofa and watch television for an hour before going upstairs as soon as they had listened to the weather report. After seven years of marriage, Virginia had considered anticipating this regular, weekly conjunction of their bodies by inserting fifty-two asterisks in her next diary, but on reflection she had decided against it. It was a little like checking the tyre pressures on the car or the oil level in the tank next to the garage. There were some things that you had to do once a week.

Virginia had originally trained to become a physiotherapist and the interest that she took in Colin's body was, in part, professional. She examined his chest for expansion, his limbs for muscle-tone, his knees and ankles for reflexes and occupied herself with a small multitude of other manifestations to ensure that he was in tip-top running order. Where there was room for improvement, she would recommend the remedial action to be taken and supervise its implementation. Even when they were making love, a small corner of her mind was monitoring the fluent deployment of the well-drilled components with the critical pride of a ballet teacher showing off her pupils at the end-of-term concert.

Every evening before Colin's shower, he would stand naked upon the bathroom scales while his wife would peer round him to see exactly where the small black arrow had come to rest. 'Ten stone, six pounds, almost a pound less than yesterday. Yes, I thought you had lost a little weight. You can get off now, dear. I have made a note of it. Not worrying about this trip are you, Colin? There's nothing to worry about. You'll be back before you know you've been away. Try some of those French cheeses when you get to Paris but make sure they are fresh. Your skin is very pale. Some sunshine would do you a power of good. What a pity you will be in the exhibition hall all day. Did you know that you've got a new mole behind your left shoulder? There used to be only two. Moles are a mild form of skin cancer, you know. We shall have to keep an eye on it. By the way, your toenails need cutting. Let's do them now.'

Colin awoke the following morning to the sound of cars swishing past on the wet road outside. It must have rained during the night. He went to the window and drew aside the white cotton curtains with their pink floral pattern. Virginia had been up for an hour already, soundlessly slipping out from the warm place in bed beside him, washing and dressing, laying the breakfast, cleaning and polishing, finishing always with the miniature ornamental glass animals on the mantelpiece in the sitting room. First she rubbed them until the rounded surfaces threw off tiny sparks of light and then she made small changes in their arrangement, finally standing back and admiring them with a little sigh of pleasure.

She heard him call out, 'The tomato soup is getting closer.' He was not speaking very clearly. He must be shaving. It was his expression for the sprawl of orange-tiled roofs that he could see from the bathroom window. There was nothing that he could do to halt its slow but inexorable march towards them. The many areas of his life over which he had no control had nurtured a certain fatalism but, as the nominal head of the household, he saw it as his duty to report regularly.

Their house was one of two semi-detached dwellings on a minor road leading south from the capital and standing like a frontier post between the edge of suburbia and a range of wooded hills that marked the beginning of open country. After breakfast they secured the doors and windows of the house, loaded the suitcase into the Fiat and set off for the station.

'I hope the train's on time, dear,' said Colin. He sat in the passenger seat clutching his briefcase to him. Now he looked at his watch and then waggled his wrist before putting the glass against his ear.

'Don't worry. I telephoned the station before we left.' She tried to keep the impatience out of her voice.

As they passed the old quarry, she slowed down to look at some children who had dropped their satchels on the grass verge and were stuffing their mouths with blackberries on their way to school.

'I might pick some blackberries at the weekend,' said Colin. 'The tree behind the house has a few nice apples on it. We could have blackberry and apple pie.'

'That would be nice,' Virginia agreed without interrupting her train of thought. When the doctors had first told her that she could never have children she had felt quite numb. It was as if she had lost a limb in an accident. The shock had driven the sensation of pain from her body leaving only a feeling of incompleteness, like an empty vase on a window sill. She often returned to that window. It was always wide open and she could see that the garden was full of flowers but they were not for picking.

Nevertheless, she must not let it ruin her life. She had to adjust. Twist her mind around. It was an expression her father used. When you could not change things, you had to twist your mind around. With a little mental dexterity you could be perfectly content with things as they were. Now, what with her new job, running the house and looking after Colin, she wondered how she would ever have found the time. Children were so demanding. They needed so much attention. If you weren't careful, they turned your life upside down. She had seen it happen.

Colin looked at his watch again. 'I'm not going to make you late for work, am I?'

'Oh no, there's lots of time.' Physiotherapy hadn't suited her. The hours at the hospital were long and you tended to become caught up in your patients' problems or they talked endlessly about their children, which she found disturbing. She had taken a typing course and an office job had led to a well-paid position as an interviewer with a secretarial agency. It was more impersonal. You didn't take the job home with you. In a year or two she should be promoted to manager.

Colin fiddled with the hasp on his briefcase and then opened it. 'I'm sure everything I need is here.'

Virginia sighed. 'Everything in your case is packed in the right order, dear. There's your train ticket, air ticket, passport, local currency, hotel booking, travellers' cheques – all in the plastic wallet. Your French phrase book is in the side flap for reading before you arrive. I have packed a small notebook in case you want to discuss business matters with Barry on the plane.'

Colin snapped the lid shut. He looked out of the window and stroked his fair, wispy moustache. Somehow he couldn't imagine Barry Wadell talking business on the plane. They both worked for a company supplying soft drinks, wines and spirits to the trade. Their main customers were hotels and public houses. Colin was a clerk in the sales office but his business cards, emblazoned with the company logo, introduced him as a Marketing Executive (Admin). He did not get out very much and there had been few opportunities to use them. For weeks on end they lay forlornly in the top drawer of his desk. Barry, a bachelor in his mid-thirties, was the company's sales representative for south-east England and, judging by the stories he told, led a buccaneering life on the open road. No publican's wife could count herself safe from this roving Lothario and by no means all of them wished to. Six months ago he had lost the seat of his trousers to an Alsatian in the back yard of a public house.

'*Two minutes earlier,*' he roared happily as he told the story to his colleagues, '*the vicious bugger would have got my underpants – and two minutes before that...*' And he waggled a huge finger at the girl behind the bar and buried his nose in a foaming tankard of the local ale. The brewery had written to his employers to complain, but Barry was a good salesman when he had his mind on his work and he escaped with a reprimand.

In recent weeks the company had entered into a joint venture with a large French group, producers of a range of table mineral waters. After consultation between the new partners, it was decided to participate in the annual Distillers and Vintners Fair in Paris, and Colin and Barry were deputed to help man the stand for the first three days. It would be a great opportunity, their sales director explained, to get to know both the product and their new French colleagues.

The car park was already packed with the cars of business people commuting to London on earlier trains so they pulled up in front of the station. Virginia signalled to a member of the railway staff that they would not be more than a minute or so and they went to the back of the car. She brushed invisible creases from her navy-blue coat and skirt as she watched her husband unload the suitcase from the boot.

Thank heavens we don't have any animals, she was thinking. A cloth like this would show every hair. She frowned with sudden irritation and stepped forward quickly. 'Colin, do try to keep the case as flat as possible.'

'I can hardly keep the case flat while I am carrying it.'

'Of course not ... but the rest of the time.'

Virginia walked with Colin to the barrier, checked with the porter that the train was on time and that they were at the right platform. Then, with a slight pursing of the lips and a narrowing of her dark-brown eyes, she looked at her watch in the brisk manner of a schoolmistress. 'You'll be at Gatwick in just under the hour. Mind you check in right away.'

Colin was subjected to a final, careful inspection. 'Your hair is a bit long, dear, but there's no time to worry about that now. Don't drink any of that French wine. You know how it disagrees with you. Look people straight in the eye and give them a firm, confident handshake.'

Colin nodded and tilted his face for a kiss. 'Goodbye, love, look after everything while I'm away.' Virginia removed her heavy tortoiseshell glasses and kissed him on the cheek. 'I'm sure it will all go well, dear. I'll see you on Wednesday evening for supper. The train times are in your briefcase – telephone me as soon as you know what time you are arriving and I'll meet you at the station.'

He watched the slim, purposeful figure until she was out of sight, her dark chestnut hair arcing from side to side as she walked. Then he crouched down to open his briefcase and extracted his train ticket.

2

In just under the hour, as his wife had predicted, Colin was standing in front of the check-in desk at Gatwick Airport. He gave his ticket to the girl and stood there shuffling his feet and fidgeting with his phrase book as he watched his luggage being weighed.

She smiled at him. 'Spot on. Twenty kilos exactly.'

'It's my wife,' he mumbled, 'she did the packing.' He grinned nervously, raising the back of his hand to his mouth as he spoke as if he felt safer talking to her over the top of a fence.

The girl was attractive and the smart dark-blue uniform set off her fair hair. She regarded him more closely. 'Have you ever flown before, Mr Loveridge?'

'No. But it doesn't worry me if that's what you're thinking.' He gave what might have been a tentative laugh but the sound emerged as a croak and once again he wiped away the noise with the back of his hand.

At that moment Colin heard his name bawled out and a blow between the shoulder blades rocked him on his feet.

'Hah! Hah! Caught you nicely, haven't I? As soon as the old cow turns her head you rope yourself a pretty little heifer...'

Colin turned around to find Barry behind him, his face red and perspiring, his mouth wide open ready to emit the braying whoop which was his trademark. Colin wrinkled his nose and turned away as he smelled on the man's breath the faint but unmistakeable aroma of cheap whisky.

The girl on the desk turned down her mouth and busied herself with some papers. Barry slapped his ticket on the counter in front of her, lowered his massive head like a bull on the point of charging and pawed the base of the desk with the toe of his shoe. The two fingers raised to the top of his ears served as horns. As for his ginger curls, they would have won a prize at a cattle show. 'Moo,' he bellowed in bovine entreaty, gazing at her from under his long, rusty eyelashes, 'Moo, moo, moo!'

The girl looked up sharply. 'That will do, Mr Wadell. It's not the first time you have flown with us, that's quite certain.' She backed away as he lurched against the counter, his arm outstretched to encircle her slim waist.

'Too right, me old darlin'. It's not my first time for anything.' Barry put his arm around his colleague and steered him unsteadily in the direction of the news-stand. What they wanted, he told Colin, was a few 'hot' magazines from off the top shelf to get them in the mood for 'Gay Paree.'

'Probably all vicars' daughters,' he confided to the world at large as he flicked through the pages before making his selection. Colin retreated to the furthest corner of the shop where he concealed his scarlet face behind a copy of *Gardening Today*. As the cries of approbation or exclamations of dismay winged their way to him, he asked himself despairingly how he could possibly survive three whole days in the company of this man.

Half an hour later they boarded the aircraft. Colin wedged his briefcase tightly under his arm as if he was a Queen's Messenger travelling with state secrets. The cabin crew returned Barry's hearty handshake with wary cordiality. In a booming, parade-ground voice which carried the length of the compartment, he enjoined his fellow passengers to 'Abandon hope all ye who enter here,' before parking his considerable bulk in a window seat, pressing all the buttons above his head and baying for a double gin and tonic.

The engines of the Boeing roared and the whole frame vibrated with pent-up energy. As the plane began its run, Colin shut his eyes and gripped the sides of his seat until his clammy fingers lost all feeling.

Barry leaned over him. 'Feeling a bit fragile, dear old thing? Why not have a noggin? It will do you a power of good.'

Colin shook his head and groaned. The nose of the plane lifted sharply and within a few seconds the roads and houses and reservoirs had shrunk to models on a town planner's board before disappearing altogether as low cloud streaked the windows with vapour and obscured the view of the ground. Each appearance of the stewardess was greeted by Barry with a jubilant war cry. He would put down his girlie magazine, roll his eyes and with his heavy ploughman's fingers, describe voluptuous arabesques in the air as he sculpted the girl's shapely figure for the benefit of his increasingly restive audience.

'If you don't behave better than this when we get to Paris,' Colin hissed at him through gritted teeth, 'you'll get us both sacked.'

With a gurgle of laughter like water running to waste, Barry subsided into his seat. Colin sighed softly. Peace at last.

But it didn't last long. Barry tapped on the seat in front of him. A face peered around at him, a middle-aged businessman, the picture of weary resignation.

'Sorry to disturb you, old chap. Can you tell me what time we're due to land at Nice?' Abruptly the face disappeared.

Colin gripped the arm of his companion. 'But surely...?'

Barry raised a finger to his lips and gave him a broad wink. 'It always unsettles them. Give him a couple of seconds and he'll ring for the stewardess. Then we'll have some fun. *See that*! What did I tell you?'

The two men made their way from Charles de Gaulle airport to their hotel by taxi. Barry flatly refused to descend to the metro. 'There are only two good reasons for going underground. Either you think there's gold down there or you don't believe in cremation.'

Colin grumbled at the expense. 'A taxi will cost the earth. Don't you think we should...?'

'Expense account, dear old thing. Put it down to the company. Where have you been all your life?'

After ten minutes' fruitless argument, Colin capitulated and they joined the queue for a taxi. On the journey Barry was a little quieter, looking out of the window, humming cheerful snatches of operetta to himself and occasionally blowing extravagant kisses to ladies he fancied as they passed by on the pavement. Their hotel was situated on the corner of the Boulevard du Montparnasse, a convenient distance from the exhibition hall. They had adjoining rooms on the first floor at the back of the building and although modest, they were quiet and comfortable.

Colin had supper by himself in the dingy dining room with its cream-painted walls and uninspiring framed prints of French provincial towns. He had expressed the desire for a quiet evening. The phrase book and a tourist map of the city were beside him. He wanted to get the feel of the place, he said. Get himself orientated.

Barry put his head round the door on his way out. 'Saving your strength for tomorrow night, dear old thing?' He fluttered a programme in his hand and Colin caught a glimpse of can-can girls and other female entertainers cavorting in varying states of undress. Then his colleague disappeared up the passage whooping and hollering like a huntsman laying his hounds on to the line as a fox breaks covert.

Colin went upstairs early. He disliked the long bolster on which he laid his head, missing the goose-feather pillows which Virginia would pat into plumpness every night before they climbed into bed. Nor did he approve of the duvet which did not tuck him in tight and snug like the big lemon-coloured double blankets they had at home. He said his prayers and tried to banish from his mind the strangeness and loneliness of it all. Mumbling French phrases to himself, at last he fell asleep.

***

The following morning at breakfast there was no sign of Barry. Colin glanced anxiously at his watch, finished his croissants, swallowed a cup of hot chocolate so quickly that it burned his throat and went upstairs again. He knocked timidly on the door for some minutes, attracting the attention of the chambermaid, who stood at the end of the corridor smiling and shaking her head. He knocked more loudly. There came a long, drawn-out groan from inside the room followed by a series of robust curses before a crumpled figure emerged hugging about him a grubby towelled dressing gown. Barry looked like a prize fighter who has gone fifteen rounds with the champion and somehow just managed to remain on his feet.

He squinted at Colin out of a single red-rimmed eye, rubbed a hand over his bristly ginger jowl and held up a warning finger. 'Not a word of reproach, dear old thing – I should blub like a baby. Be a sport and get a big glass of fresh orange juice and a jug of black coffee sent up. Don't bother about French ... just shout in English. The natives only *pretend* they can't understand. Fifteen minutes grace and I shall be a new man – *and then, Paris, watch out for Barry*!'

Against all the odds, after a great scramble and an alarming taxi ride, they arrived on time at the exhibition hall, a vast, modern, glass and steel edifice, designed in the style of a huge marquee. Barry insisted that they did a quick 'recce' before reporting for duty. He strode up and down the aisles, peering from side to side, viewing the hospitality tents, the uncorked bottles and polished glasses with mounting enthusiasm. 'It's an alcoholic's dream of paradise, old sport. *Freebies galore!*'

Colin had stopped at a stand to pick up a brochure. He felt that it would make a good impression on Mr Cordery, the sales director, if he arrived back with some information on the local competition. Suddenly he found himself alone. Panic-stricken at being abandoned, he hared back the way they had come. To his huge relief he found Barry on the stand of a well-known company of wine shippers. The stand was decked out with white Versailles tubs brimful of flowers. Red, white and blue streamers ran from a maypole in the centre to the four corners of the display area. Secretaries in white blouses and elegant navy-blue skirts bustled to and fro. Miracles of chic, Colin thought them.

Barry was in the middle of a small group of senior executives, all immaculately turned out in dark, well-cut business suits. He had a glass of red wine in his hand and was holding it up to the light. There was a pause of a few seconds and then his nose, ripe as a July strawberry, snuffed at the rim for the bouquet. Another pause before he tipped the juices lovingly over his palate. His eyes rolled heavenward. 'The jewel in the Burgundian crown,' he pronounced with a wet, noisy kiss to his fingertips. He would have said more, but frantic signals from Colin persuaded him otherwise and with a flourish of the now empty glass and a deep bow to his rapt little audience, he took his leave.

'The French are convinced that all Englishmen are mad,' he said to Colin as he rejoined him. 'Take it from me, old thing, it is the greatest mistake to disappoint them.'

***

In the space of a few days, Barry's flamboyant figure became something of a showpiece. People looked out for Monsieur Barry with his windmilling arms and hustling, fairground barker's manner, his canary-yellow waistcoat with its shiny brass buttons stretched across the bow of his ample belly, the silk handkerchief running like a red river from the breast pocket of his blazer or hauled out to mop the perspiration from his glistening forehead.

Visitors drifting down the aisles were not permitted to shuffle past him in that sleepwalker's trance which is the despair of the exhibitor. Barry cajoled, flattered and abused them by turns, taking little runs at them, nudging them this way and that like a Welsh collie with a flock of awkward sheep, finally driving them into the pen where the salesmen waited with their wry smiles and cynical faces, order books in hand, ready to pounce.

Colin sheltered in the lee of his large colleague. His emotions were a jumble of pride, embarrassment and apprehension, his face twitching with nervous goodwill as he handed out leaflets or put a hand on Wadell's arm to restrain his wilder gesticulations and the loud, inconsequential cries of *'Formidable! Ravissant!'* Or, in moments of chagrin, *'Infame! Absolument infame!'*

3

That evening, Barry insisted, they must go to *Le Diable*, a nightclub of which friends in the rugby team had spoken approvingly. Colin's protestations that it would be too expensive and, anyway, he was a married man were overborne. 'I will brook no argument, dear old thing. The very thought of you languishing in bed with a French phrase book for company when every pretty filly in Paris is dying to half-mast her knickers for the English milord is enough to make a chap burst into tears.'

They had dinner first in a brasserie in the Place Blanche, pushing their way through the noise and the cigarette smoke to find an empty table. The waiters in their black jackets and long white aprons flew around the room like wasps in a jam factory, disappearing every few moments through the swing doors leading to the kitchen. They emerged again balancing steaming plates on their upturned hands, rocking and swaying with wonderful verve and precision among the heads of the diners. Round-eyed and open-mouthed, Colin sat in his chair like a child with a ringside seat at the circus.

Barry was soon on first-name terms with their waiter. 'My friend is painfully thin, Gaston,' he said mournfully. He sounded like an anxious mother who has taken her son to the doctor. 'Look at him, all dick and ribs like a gypsy dog.' Colin's look of reproach was rewarded with a long hoot of laughter.

The waiter smiled uncomprehendingly. 'Would Monsieur Dick care for *un bifteck avec pommes frites et champignons?*'

Barry gave a great yelp of delight. '*Monsieur Dick* ...' he gasped, 'Gaston, that is simply marvellous.' He wiped his eyes. '*Bien sûr*, a beef steak with all the trimmings.' With his hands he mimed a gargantuan helping. '*Tout de suite* for Monsieur Dick. I'll have the same.'

After fortifying himself with two glasses of Côtes du Rhône, Barry subjected the other diners to the most searching scrutiny before pronouncing the restaurant a notorious place of assignation. 'There's no doubt about it,' and he pointed an accusing finger at the complacent figures lining the long rows of crimson plush banquettes. '*Just look at them*! Philanderers with their fancy ladies. The place is a scandal. It ought to be closed down!'

'I can't see any...' Colin confessed after a careful survey of the room. He felt rather out of his depth.

'*Can't see any!* Why, they are as thick as starlings on a telegraph pole!' He pointed with his knife at the objects of his allegations in a gesture reminiscent of a farmer at a provincial cattle market.

Colin sipped his wine, tentatively at first. Virginia would not have approved ... but she could be a little narrow-minded at times ... and then, growing bolder, drained the glass. 'What about the pair opposite?' he whispered, pointing at a stylish, middle-aged woman in the company of a man with the dark, dangerous looks of a young Alain Delon.

'*Amour bébé,* ' Barry decreed, looking up from his well-laden plate. 'He can't be more than eighteen.'

Colin, perplexed, put down his knife and fork. 'What do you mean?'

'You see her companion?'

'Yes. Is he her son?'

A howl of disdain greeted this suggestion. *'Her son!'* Barry removed the huge napkin tucked into his collar and wiped his mouth. 'This is Paris, dear old thing, not Padstow. Let me put you right. The lady in question is a rich, experienced older woman. Her husband, if he's still with us, is long past it. He probably takes pills to get upstairs. So she has a problem, a big, big problem. And what does she do? She finds herself a handsome young lover, flatters him, buys him nice clothes and teaches him to make the best of himself. And what does he do for her? Well, that's obvious, isn't it? He's much cheaper than a month at a health farm and probably more fun. And it's wonderful what a little *'eau de vie'* will do to smooth away the wrinkles. When she's sixty she won't look a day over forty. See how she toys with the salmon mousse while he wolfs down a dozen oysters. She has to keep her figure. He's got to keep his strength up.'

'Good Lord!' said Colin.

At that moment, a gypsy woman entered the restaurant, her long black hair and handsome Romany features half-hidden behind an armful of red roses. With little swirls of her dress and light, nimble movements, she proceeded to do a round of the tables.

'Watch this! *This will flush them out!'* cried Barry, bouncing up and down on his seat. 'Now let's see who is curling up after dinner with a hot water bottle – and who isn't!' They watched closely while the fate of the roses was decided. Colin, flushed in the face, entered into the spirit of the thing. Gallantry was rewarded with gleeful cries of, *'See that!* I told you so!' The purchase of several roses was greeted with shouts of, *'Simply flagrant!'* but Barry blew loud raspberries at those diners who waved the flower seller away. 'Old miseries!' he said scornfully and the two toasted each other in glass after glass of red wine.

'Et comme dessert?' enquired Gaston gravely. He liked to see people enjoy themselves but the two Englishmen had drunk too much and were over-boisterous. The English were mean, stingy when it came to tipping. He would load their bill a little. They would never notice a discreet supplement tucked away among the scrawl of figures. 'Monsieur Dick would find the rum baba most agreeable...'

Barry looked at his companion and nodded. They would both have rum baba. 'And, Gaston, two cognacs to follow.' He leaned back and belched contentedly.

After dinner the two men walked up the boulevard towards the Place Pigalle. The cinemas were emptying and the pavements crowded with people strolling home or sitting at café tables beneath awnings which had once been bold reds and greens but were now dull and faded. Colin gave quick, darting glances to the side, up the dimly lit, narrow alleys which mounted to Montmartre where under a full moon the Basilica of the Sacré Coeur in its marble nakedness presided over the warm autumn evening like a white goddess.

The women on the corners of the streets who beckoned him with their crimson, lacquered mouths and unenigmatic gestures of invitation repelled and excited him. The pimps in their black leather jackets with their oily hair and savage, pockmarked faces appalled him but stirred him also. It was thrilling to be ambling in this carefree manner and yet be so close to such viciousness, to feel that he had only to step into the shadowy side streets to cross an unmarked frontier and find himself in a foreign country, a land of unimaginable violence and sensuality.

Colin felt strangely light-headed. He scarcely heard the wolf whistles and cock crows from Barry who halted every few paces outside the clubs to examine lurid photographs of the 'artistes' with their contortionist poses and surrealist breasts and buttocks or to catechise the doormen in his vigorous schoolboy French. His broad, unambiguous mime was reinforced with conspiratorial leers and winks punctuated with great whoops of laughter.

Colin's head was turning around like the neon-lit sails of the Moulin Rouge. The hubbub, the glitter and dazzle seemed to run in his blood like a fever. It was the same intoxicating mixture of elation and fear that had seized him once many years before. It happened shortly after his fourteenth birthday. He had awakened in the middle of the night trembling all over. He ran to the bathroom fearing that he must be ill. His pyjamas were damp with sweat and, as he stripped, spasm after spasm overwhelmed his body. The sensations were so powerful that he had been driven up against the door where, half-fainting, he had to hold himself against the woodwork to prevent himself from falling. Now, for the first time since that night, he felt within himself the same potentiality, believed himself on the brink of an extraordinary adventure, an experience that would unravel his nature and like the passing of a great storm, leave the landscape changed forever. He was in an ecstasy of alarm.

An illuminated sign attached to the side of a tall, narrow building showed that they had arrived at *Le*

Diable. Catching sight of his reflection in a window, Colin squared his narrow shoulders, drilled his drooping moustache and passed a hand over the sparse strands of hair that trailed across the bald patch at the back of his head. A flight of steps under a low awning led down to the entrance to the club.

Barry paused on the first step and regarded his companion. 'I must say, you look damned odd. Are you sure that you feel alright?'

Colin returned a blank, unfocused stare. 'I feel tremendous. Simply tremendous.'

Encouraged, Barry padded down the steps and pressed the bell on the door. The door opened just enough to permit an exchange of whispers with the mystery voice behind it, then a little wider to allow four fingers to appear, grasp a crumpled note and disappear before it swung open to admit them. As they pushed through a bead curtain, Colin put a hand on Barry's arm to steady himself. He heard his companion cry out, 'Champagne! *Lots of it!* And a table at the front ... near the action ... your two best birds ... *Vive La France!*'

4

Colin remembered very little more until the following morning when he sat up rigid with the shock of cold water splashed in his face and found Barry standing over him with an empty glass in his hand. 'It's time to wake up, Monsieur Dick. We've got to be on the stand in an hour.'

Colin groaned. 'Just leave me alone and for heaven's sake stop calling me Monsieur Dick.' He sank back again into the bed, pulling the sheet to his chin. Through half-closed eyes he watched Barry, stupefied with merriment, circling the room performing what looked like an Apache war dance while keeping up a low chant interspersed with little choking sounds.

At last, overcome, Barry wiped his streaming eyes with the back of his hands and sat down on the edge of the bed. 'Dear Lord!' he sobbed. 'What a night! If you could ... if you could have seen yourself ... with Miss ... with Miss Black Magic ... from Guadeloupe.'

Colin opened his eyes and sat up in bed. Affecting an insouciance he was far from feeling, he said slowly, 'I don't remember anything. Did she come to our table?'

Barry doubled up over his knees. *'Come to our table!'* he roared. 'I should just think she did. You great clown! *You spent half the frigging night with her!'*

Colin, clad in vest and underpants, hurled himself from his bed. *'What!'* he shrieked. 'I don't believe it. It's not possible!'

Barry collapsed on the bed, flopping about helplessly like a fish in the bottom of a boat. 'Not only possible, dear old thing, but an accomplished fact. What is more, I almost needed a mechanical grab to tear you from the lady's delightful and very ample bosom. It was five in the morning when I got you back here, preserving what little remained of your modesty, as you can see.'

Colin crossed the room and stared at himself in the mirror. He half-expected not to recognise himself, to find his features reconstructed like a house rebuilt after an earthquake. His limbs ached and his back felt as if he had sunburn. He longed for Barry to leave the room so that he could remove his underclothes and examine himself.

'Where did you spend the night?' He was not interested in the answer. He was thinking of Black Magic, the sorceress to whom he had entrusted his body during those long, unconscious hours of darkness.

Barry was lounging back on the bed. He closed his eyes and smiled. 'With the nubile Babette! A lady with as many turns as an anaconda. She and Black Magic were stable companions. They shared a flat in the Rue Clichy and if you can recall the rooms – well, stable is the word for it.'

Colin filled the basin with hot water and quickly set out his shaving things. 'Barry, tell me – what was Black Magic really like?'

'You swear you can't remember?'

'Very little. We must have arrived in the middle of the floor show. We had a table right at the front. There was a man dressed as a fisherman.'

'Ah, that was Pedro. Rather improbably attired in a cat mask, a thong which looked liked David's catapult before he took that shy at Goliath, and a black furry tail.'

'Yes. I do remember that ... and there was a giant goldfish bowl.'

'Containing a human goldfish – a delectable redhead with a fishtail of golden sequins – and her own unforgettable version of the breaststroke. Pedro dangled his hook into the water. It fastened onto her tail. She struggled to get away. *Oh! It was simply wonderful!*'

Colin ran a hand over his chin. It was like trying to remember a dream the next morning. 'Two girls came to our table. One had gold bangles from her wrist to halfway up her arm ... and huge earrings.'

'That was Black Magic. Her skin was superb – as shiny as a stick of liquorice. She had lips as red as a fresh watermelon. As for her figure...' Barry described voluptuous curves in the air. 'And a derrière that a man would sell his soul for – you lucky dog!'

Colin removed his vest and lathered his face. Barry had started to say that they should hurry but stopped in mid-sentence. He ignored the half-stifled moans and groans that came from his direction. He disliked stripping in the presence of a stranger. Barry probably thought he was a poor physical specimen. Despite all Virginia's efforts, he was rather scrawny. But what of it? We can't all be made like Hercules. He despised Barry. The man was coarse-grained. Vulgar. But he admired him also and coveted his membership of that freemasonry of men of the world to which he seemed so effortlessly to belong.

He picked up the razor. It didn't seem to have occurred to Barry that he must have passed out on Black Magic's bed. He could hardly have been in a condition to have done anything else. But Barry must never know that. He must be encouraged to think the best of him. If that was the sum of the adventure, it achieved a very happy balance. He could count himself a member of Barry's fraternity at no more burden to his conscience than a pennyweight or so.

He couldn't conceive of life with Virginia with even a ripple of suspicion between them. He simply would not be able to cope. He was a poor actor and an unimaginative, incompetent liar. How could it be otherwise? Dissembling took practice and he had never given Virginia reason to doubt him. His wife may have had no sixth sense but she more than made up for it with the other five. It made him anxious. Fortunately, as things had turned out, the fraying of the bond of fidelity had been very slight. As they lay down together on Saturday night, even Virginia would not be able to detect that his spirit level was a degree or so out of true.

He finished shaving, dabbed the tips of his fingers with the aftershave, patted his cheeks and gave the ends of his moustache a playful twist. He squared his shoulders and addressed the mirror with studied indifference. 'I was very drunk last night but I expect I managed well enough.'

Barry pushed the pillow off his face. 'All things considered, dear old thing ...' he managed to gasp, 'I think you managed splendidly.'

Colin turned to look at him. Barry was rolling from one side of the bed to the other, hugging himself with his powerful arms, tears of uncontrollable laughter streaming from his eyes. A strangled sound came from him. 'Have you seen your back ... Monsieur Dick ... it looks as if Black Magic has gone over you with a disc harrow!' Another convulsion seized him and he brought his knees up to his chest, grabbed at a corner of the sheet and thrust it into his mouth.

'*What do you mean?*' Colin whirled around to catch sight of his back in the mirror. It was true. From his shoulders to his loins his pallid skin was scored with long, thin red lines. In places the scratches were smudged with dried bloodstains. His face turned as white as the walls of the room. '*What is it?*' he screamed. 'Have I caught something from her? Or did she attack me? For God's sake, Barry, you've got to tell me! What's happened to me!'

Barry had hauled a blanket over his head. Now he emerged purple in the face and wheezing like an asthmatic. 'Put it down to experience, dear old thing. A wound received in the lists of love. The lady's flail to your lance. Monsieur Dick ...' he gasped, 'Monsieur Dick must be very passionate.'

Colin rushed to examine his vest, turning it inside out, fingering the faint stains, now brown and faded, on the material. 'How could she do this to me, Barry? *How could she?* She did this ... with her nails? Good God, man, she must have claws like a cat!'

Barry pushed himself off the bed and came over to Colin. He put his arm round his shoulders. He had managed to straighten his face but his blue eyes danced with merriment. 'Black Magic was overwhelmed, Colin ... quite overcome ... it was as if you had launched a torpedo into a fireworks factory.' He spread his arms wide. '*Boom!* Black Magic couldn't help herself. It should make you very proud.'

But Colin wasn't listening.

5

Barry had to pack for Colin, who had seemed incapable of co-ordinating mind and body. He paid the hotel bill and since they were late and carrying their suitcases, they took a taxi. The exhibition hall was as crowded as on the previous day. Colin handed out his leaflets but his movements were listless and mechanical. From time to time his lips moved soundlessly and his eyes strayed to the big clock above the gangway leading to the first floor.

Their flight was at half-past seven. In no more than a few hours they would be landing in England. Allowing for the change in time, he would be home by ... but his brain had seized like the engine of a car starved of oil and refused to do the calculation. He prayed for deliverance. Without a vestige of hope that his petition would be answered, he prayed that he might be taken ill or knocked down by a car or attacked in the street. Any calamity so long as it delayed his departure or disguised the origin of his extraordinary injuries.

He cursed the unbroken harmony of seven years of marriage. Other couples had shouting matches, threw plates, practised the grossest deceptions on each other. Agonising quarrels, passionate reconciliation. These were the staple of any normal marriage. Virginia and he had been wantonly, recklessly faithful to one another. The comfortable little ark that they had built together was fine for a light shower of rain but not for the deluge that was coming. It would sink them.

Barry came up to him. 'You look like an advertisement for an embalming parlour,' he hissed. 'Go and sit inside the office if you don't feel well.

You're frightening my customers.' Barry had a hangover and his usual ebullience had deserted him.

Colin glared at him but made no answer. From where he was standing he could keep his eye on the clock, could calculate with appalling precision exactly how many minutes remained to him before his life tipped over a precipice. He tried to picture himself stepping onto the bathroom scales, Virginia starting to run the shower, testing it for temperature; then she would turn and come over to him to take the reading. He, standing there ... in all his nakedness ... with the lacerations on his back crying to high heaven for vengeance. He closed his eyes. His mind refused to transmit the images of the unthinkable, the unimaginable. He could as soon conceive of himself sweeping the ornamental glass animals that Virginia cherished and polished every day off the mantelpiece and into the fireplace. Smashing every one.

At five o'clock, the directors and staff squeezed into the small office in the centre of the stand. The sales director made a brief speech of thanks to his *chers collègues* before presenting them with a company tie and a presentation pack of mineral water. The two men, subdued but for different reasons, shook hands all round, collected their baggage and set off for the airport.

'Mineral water,' Barry grumbled, 'four lousy bottles of mineral water. Tight-fisted frog-eaters.' Then, looking at his colleague, 'I say, you don't look very bright. Are you sure you are well enough to travel?'

'What am I going to do?' moaned Colin. *'What on earth am I going to do?'*

'Do?' Barry looked at him blankly. He frowned as he ran his hand through his curly hair and then remembered. 'Oh, that. You don't want to let things like that get you down. Carry it off with a bit of style. Tell the old lady she had better look to her laurels or you'll be off to Paris every weekend.' He gave a little yelp of glee. He was beginning to feel jollier, more like his old self again. Colin was a good chap but he was rather a wet blanket. This sort of trip wasn't his form. He would have been much happier back in the office with the other pencil pushers. He sighed contentedly. The prospect of putting his fist round a tankard of decent ale was cheering. Wine was all very well but you couldn't beat a good Kentish beer.

He would drive Colin home. The poor fellow didn't look very chipper and it wasn't more than twenty minutes out of his way. He would stop off at the Bird In Hand on the way. Harry, the publican, had been hurt by a heavy aluminium keg falling on him and wasn't the man he used to be. Jackie, his wife, was single-handed and finding it difficult to cope. He'd stay on after closing time ... help Jackie clear up. In life, one thing very often led to another.

Mile after mile, Colin stared unseeingly out of the taxi window. As the taxi turned into the airport, he turned to Barry with an air of resolution. 'I can't go home,' he declared. 'Not possibly.' Then, plaintively, 'May I stay with you, Barry? *Please, Barry?*'

'No, you can't,' Barry retorted. 'It's out of the question.' Then, more kindly, 'Look, Colin, women are all the same. They make one hell of a fuss if they catch you with your leg over but secretly they think you're twice the chap. Buy the old girl a big bottle of scent at the duty-free and buck up, for Pete's sake. *You're being a bore!'*

***

Virginia was sitting at her desk flicking through the pages of the previous year's diary. She switched on the lamp. It was early October and at half-past seven the light was no more than a glimmer in the western sky. They had gone to Twin Pines again that summer. Perhaps next year they would be ready for a change, for something slightly different. The little seaside town was quiet, charming in its own way, but it wasn't very 'stretching'. She would talk to Colin about it. It was almost a year since her company had sent her to Tunbridge Wells on a training course. Self-assertiveness, the latest management importation from the United States, had been the keynote. When she had returned home at the end of the week, she had been remodelled. Her hair, which used to fall below her shoulders, had been chopped to half its length and her nail varnish and lipstick were in aggressively bright colours. She had bought the dark-blue coat and skirt for work and purchased the heavy tortoiseshell spectacles.

In November, she paid her last visit to the specialist. He was sorry. There was nothing that he could do for her. Had she and her husband considered adopting a child? No, they hadn't. In a way their tiny household had become her family. She found herself picking up objects in the house, running her hands along the surfaces and down the edges like a blind person, as if very gradually she would learn to feel again, as if through the tips of her fingers an infinitely precious, long-lost sensation would be restored to her. Colin and the house, they had been her salvation, the diary her life raft. She had stocked it well, laid in provisions, for the shipwrecked sailor had no way of knowing how long the voyage would be.

Virginia looked at her watch and frowned. It was inconsiderate of Colin not to have telephoned from the airport, and most unlike him. She had called Flight Enquiries to learn that the plane from Paris would be landing a little ahead of schedule. Even if he was getting a lift home in Barry's car, as now seemed probable, she would have liked to know exactly when to expect him. Knowing Barry's habits, he would probably want to stay for a drink. She would have put out the best glasses. Fortunately there was a bottle of Spanish white wine in the refrigerator.

Colin knew that she could not bear uncertainty. So far as possible she had planned uncertainty out of their existence. But sometimes Colin liked to fabricate little mysteries and then surprise her. It was a quirk in him that she didn't care for. She had done with mysteries. She detested them. Mysteries were untidy. They were subversive. To her they seemed slightly degenerate.

***

'Cheer up, dear old thing,' Barry whispered when they were airborne. 'Your face reminds me of the blancmange they used to give us at school.' He had ordered half a bottle of champagne and was chuckling his way through a book of strip cartoons that he had purchased at the airport, a work of undisguised pornography.

Colin was falling apart. He had one gin and tonic after the other. Tears ran down his cheeks as he thought of his beloved Virginia. Virginia welcoming him home, Virginia preparing his supper, Virginia turning down the sheets on the bed, putting out his pyjamas, Virginia holding him tight after they made love on Saturday night, the shyly whispered endearments before they went to sleep. How gallant she was, how brave and uncomplaining. Her husband and the sparkling little home they shared were her whole life. Virginia was not close to her mother. She had no brothers or sisters. She had no children to tend and nurture, no future in their hearts and memories when she was gone. And he had betrayed her. Betrayed her with a tart in a sordid back street that he couldn't find his way back to if he tried. Why, he didn't even know the woman's real name. A teardrop splashed onto his hand.

Barry looked up from his book. 'You look a right old mess.' He belched noisily and then leaned across the gangway to address the woman on his left. 'What's your name, gorgeous? Are you doing anything tonight?'

'My name,' she replied smoothly, running a hand through her heavily bleached hair but not raising her eyes from her magazine, 'is none of your business. And I am doing something tonight.'

Barry leered at her, his eyes bright with lust and Lanson Black Label. 'I bet you are, sweetheart, but why not do it with me?'

She snapped the magazine shut, almost taking off the end of his nose. 'Look, Mister Whoever-you-are, go and piss in another pot. I only play with big boys. *You don't even make the Colts.*'

The captain's voice came over the intercom. They should fasten their seat belts ready for landing at Gatwick in ten minutes.

Discomforted only for a moment, Barry reached into his pocket and produced a plastic deodorant container. He passed it round the corner of the seat in front of him. 'Anyone want to give their armpits a birthday? Pass it along.'

Colin wiped his eyes and blew his nose. He closed the folding table in front of him and handed his glass to the stewardess. He had reached a decision and with that knowledge, a great calm came over him. He was ready to purge his corrupt and sinful body, to expiate the sins of the Rue Clichy. That the path he had chosen meant great suffering he was in no doubt.

They loaded the cases into the boot of Barry's car at the airport's multi-storey car park and set off on their journey across country. Barry drove through the narrow lanes with the speed and confidence of a man who has been drinking but is not drunk. As they approached a major road, a police car raced past in front of them, its red and blue lights flashing in the darkness. A loudspeaker mounted on the roof was blaring an announcement. They both wound down their windows but were unable to catch the words.

'Probably giving the winner of the last race at Lingfield,' Barry joked. Colin didn't reply and his companion gave him a curious glance. 'Not still fussing about the little woman are you, dear old thing? Don't give it another thought. This adventure will spice up married life no end. You'll see. There's nothing like a bit of competition to keep the girls on their toes – or rather, off their toes, if you take my meaning.' He chortled happily.

It was now quite dark. Barry shifted in his seat and the car slowed. 'We'll be there in five minutes. Will you be alright or do you want me to come in ... crack a few jokes ... warm up the old bird a bit?'

'No. Drop me by the quarry. It's just around the corner. It's only a couple of hundred yards from the house. I'll walk from there.' Colin put his hand on his companion's arm. 'Thanks, Barry. I know you've tried to help.' He spoke so strangely, his voice seemed to have fallen down a mineshaft.

Barry was alarmed. 'You sound like something out of the spirit world, old thing. You're not thinking of doing anything foolish?'

They drove in silence until Colin said, 'This will do,' and Barry swung the car across the road and into a lay-by. To their right, in the glare of the headlights they could see a narrow grass verge bounded by thick bramble rising to waist height. It was impossible to judge the width of this belt of bramble for it rolled away into the darkness and beyond it the quarry was no more than a glimmer where the limestone face rose sheer to the wooded hillside above.

For a moment Colin sat without moving. He was very pale and his face was damp with perspiration. He seized Barry's hand and shook it. Then quickly he opened the door of the car and jumped out. 'Thank you for everything, Barry,' he said. 'I think you ought to go now.' He went round to the back and opened the boot.

Barry looked into his rear mirror but his view was obstructed by the raised lid of the boot. A moment later he heard the snap of the boot being shut. He put the car into gear and was moving forward when from somewhere across the dark fields he heard once more the sound of the loudspeaker. The words were being spoken slowly and emphatically but he was unable to make any sense of them above the noise of the engine. He turned the ignition switch and wound down his window to hear better. At that moment, he glanced in his wing mirror.

Colin had removed his coat and tie and the buttons of his white shirt must have been undone, for the garment hung loosely about him. His suitcase and the small black briefcase lay at the edge of the road. He had crossed the grass verge and stood pressed right up against the briars with his back to him. In the red glow of the rear lights, the shirt looked as if it was soaked in blood. The dark purple stems with their needle-sharp thorns criss-crossed each other like coils of barbed wire, the top strands curling around his waist. Barry had opened his mouth to shout when Colin raised his arms to shoulder height and toppled forward, falling in a straight line like a tree that has been felled, down into the thick bramble.

Colin did not close his eyes. He would spare himself nothing. *Dear God! How he was prepared to suffer!* For a moment the top layers supported him and the pain was endurable but he could feel the blood running down his cheeks and the palms of his hands. Then, as he started to sink, there came a rustling in the undergrowth immediately below him. Colin found himself staring into a pair of enormous green eyes.

Half mad with terror, in that millionth of a second, he knew that he was face to face with Sin itself. Satan had come for him. There was a tearing sound as the

Thing sprang out at him, its fetid, slaughterhouse breath hot on his face, catching him a glancing blow on the shoulder, spinning him around. And now he was falling again, the thorns tugging at him, piercing his skin through the tattered shirt, tearing at him and then releasing him to the layers below, as the weight of his body bore him down to the shallow floor of the quarry.

6

It was not far short of midnight but there was still a large crowd in front of the county town's general hospital. Arc lights had been set up in the forecourt and many of the police cars had their headlights full on. Flashbulbs were popping off every few seconds. A short, plump man in a double-breasted suit was standing at the top of a wide flight of steps. He was speaking from a sheet of paper that he held in front of him and shielding his eyes from the glare with his free hand.

Barry shook hands with a small group of reporters who tucked their notebooks into their pockets as they turned away. He walked a few yards to his car and then stopped to listen to the speaker who had finished reading from his notes and was now taking questions.

'Yes, the tiger can be a dangerous and unpredictable animal – and particularly when frightened. The police? They did a splendid job. Warning? The public received repeated warnings to report sightings but on no account to approach the animal. Her name? She's called Sheba. No, we haven't been able to speak to Mr Loveridge. He's heavily sedated and short visits from close members of his family are all that the nursing staff will permit.'

'Where is Mr Wadell?' someone in the crowd called out.

'The police have taken a full statement from him.'

There was a shout from another. 'How did Mr Loveridge spot the animal?'

'It seems that Sheba was hiding in thick undergrowth at the side of the road. We understand that

Mr Loveridge was in a car. He just saw her eyes. They would have shown up very clearly in the headlights. He went to investigate.'

'Was Mr Loveridge in any danger?' someone at the back cried out.

The speaker pulled a large handkerchief from his pocket and wiped his forehead. 'Well, I think I have already answered that. Let me add that his action was very courageous and public-spirited but he would have done better to report the sighting to the police or ourselves. A reward? I believe that I can speak for my fellow directors in saying that we shall be sending Mr Loveridge a token of our gratitude in recognition of his brave action.'

'How did Sheba escape?' a man called out from the edge of the crowd.

'We have investigated this very thoroughly. It appears that a large branch of a tree close to the perimeter broke off and, through sheer bad luck, fell against the fence. Sheba walked up the branch and jumped over the other side. It was a wholly exceptional occurrence.' There was a murmur from his audience and he felt constrained to continue. 'As a director of the Northdown Animal Kingdom, I should emphasise that the creatures in our care enjoy a great deal of freedom,' there was laughter at this, 'and we pride ourselves that we give them a habitat as close to that of nature as is practicable. But I must emphasise that the safety of the public remains paramount.'

A woman waved a newspaper, trying to catch his eye. 'Can you tell us – how long did it take you to catch her?'

'No more than twenty minutes from the time Mr Wadell called. She was padding up the lane when we found her. Probably on her way home. I expect she was hungry and wanted her supper. Photographs? The press have been issued with photographs. We may take some more pictures of Sheba later on tomorrow. Let her sleep off the effects of the tranquilliser dart.' He buttoned his jacket and put away his notes. 'One last question and then let's all get off home to bed. It's been a long day.'

'Was Mr Loveridge badly mauled, Sir?' a reporter asked.

The speaker turned to the houseman standing beside him and they conferred for a moment. 'I understand,' he said, facing his audience once more, 'that no bulletin on Mr Loveridge's condition will be issued before midday tomorrow at the earliest.'

There was another whispered conference before the houseman stepped forward, a tired-eyed young man in a long white coat. 'I am able to confirm that Mr Loveridge has some lacerations to the body but his condition is as comfortable as could be expected under the circumstances.'

***

The next morning, Barry telephoned his office to say that he was going to visit Colin at the hospital and would be late in to work. As regards their joint exploits, he could add very little to what they would have read in the newspapers. Colin and Sheba had made the headlines in several local papers and they were on the front page of two of the nationals.

He drove to the hospital and found Virginia and the ward sister at Colin's bedside.

'Mr Barry ... ah, well since you're Mr Colin's friend.' The nurse turned and smiled as she reached the door. 'I have just changed his dressings. Now he needs as much rest as possible, so don't stay too long.' The door closed softly behind her.

Virginia rose from her chair and clasped Barry's hands between her own. Tears of pride shone in her large brown eyes. 'Colin is quite the hero, isn't he?' There had been a message from the Mayor, the local radio station wanted to interview him, people from television, newspaper reporters. For a moment she was overwhelmed by it all and turned away, gazing around the room with its cards, flowers and baskets of fruit while she reached in her bag for a handkerchief.

Barry nodded. 'Yes, he's a real celebrity.' He followed the direction of her eyes. 'It's quite amazing – like the Chelsea Flower Show.' He gave a muted whoop but seeing Virginia's reproachful frown, quickly put a hand over his mouth. He went over to the side of the bed and stood looking down at the patient. 'Has he spoken at all?' he asked, trying to keep his voice casual.

'No. The poor darling hasn't said a word. He's still heavily sedated.' She looked at her husband with something like awe. Softly, almost to herself, she whispered, 'Just imagine! Colin grappling with that ... *that terrifying wild beast!*'

Colin was lying on his side. His face, what could be seen of it for swathes of bandages, was very pale against the blue linen pillow. Barry reached into his briefcase, extracted several of the day's newspapers and placed them beside the bed. He looked troubled.

Virginia stepped up to him and with a shy smile, kissed him on the cheek. It was sweet of Barry to be so concerned. She almost found it in her heart to forgive him for leading Colin into such danger.

'When Colin wakes up,' Barry said to her, 'he may seem frightened and confused. When people are in shock they can behave very strangely, say odd things. You will be here, won't you, to explain very quietly and gently what has happened to him?'

Virginia smiled at him. Barry really was a dear. He had sides to him that she had never suspected. How she had misjudged him. It took a crisis like this to discover what people were really like. 'Don't worry,' she assured him, 'I will be here, at his side, when he wakes up.'

She looked down at Colin and a single tear ran slowly down her cheek. His face looked so pinched. 'Naughty boy, he has lost quite a lot of weight.' Preoccupied for a moment with her own thoughts, she was silent. Then she smiled and her brown eyes sparkled. 'But we'll soon make that up.'

The Nightingale

Once upon a time in the not-so-far-off future, a girl called Carrie lived with her father and mother in an old farmhouse on the east coast of America. Chet, her dad, had always wanted to be a farmer, grow a few crops and keep some cows but he had taken flying lessons for fun and had shown such aptitude that his instructors told him that he should train to be a pilot.

Chet was not keen to do this but his wife Beth won him over. They would be much better off, she told him. Carrie could go to a good school and they could take nice holidays and run a big car and still be able to put money aside for their old age.

Chet was a natural pilot and rapid promotion followed. After a few years there came the day when he was told that he was to be the captain of a new space rocket. Travel in space had reached the point when these rockets carried hundreds of passengers to the moon and beyond.

The latest rocket was a marvel of science. In the cabin there were myriads of dials and switches to enable the pilot to guide and control the rocket and only a very few people had all the qualities required to do the job.

Carrie was growing up to be a normal, boisterous, sometimes noisy girl, but on her seventh birthday all that was to change. Her father returned from his first commercial flight in the rocket and went straight to bed, exhausted. Carrie was having a tea party for her friends and, at her mother's insistence, they were sent home early.

Beth took her daughter into the garden and they sat in the shade of the large cedar tree that grew beside the house. 'Carrie, my dear,' her mother began, 'listen to me carefully and heed all that I say. Your father is very tired. The strain of piloting the new rocket and being responsible for the lives of all those people is very great. When he comes home, he must have absolute peace and quiet so that he can recover his strength and be at his best when he flies again.

'So from now on you must always keep your voice low and move around the house quietly and not drop your toys on the floor. It will not be easy, Carrie, but your father's work brings us many good things and we must be prepared to make sacrifices. Will you promise me this, my daughter?'

A tear rolled slowly down Carrie's cheek. 'But Mother,' she whispered, 'Father is not always here. When he is away, can I not laugh and sing and ask my friends to come here and play?'

Her mother put an arm around her but she shook her head. 'I am so sorry, my dear,' she replied, 'I know it is hard, but unless you discipline yourself in this way, one day you may forget. Then your father will not get all the rest he needs and when he goes back to work, he may still be tired. Before he launches the rocket, he has to run through his long checklist. Perhaps he will miss one of the items. There could be a terrible accident and hundreds of people – people who have entrusted themselves to your father – could lose their lives.'

Carrie taught herself to speak so softly that the words were hardly more than a whisper. When she went to school, she was given a desk at the front of the class so that the teacher could hear her. At home, she used to take her shoes off and walk through the rooms in her stockinged feet. Even if she hurt herself, she learned not to call out.

Several years passed. The house was now so quiet that the birds, accustomed to the laughter of children, no longer visited the garden. The nightingale that used to perch on a branch opposite her parents' bedroom window and sing during the hours of darkness flew away. Carrie's friends never came to see her. The place seemed so sad and gloomy that they did not feel like playing games. Even the flowers looked drab and sickly and lost their bright colours.

Sometimes, when she was tossing and turning and unable to get to sleep, Carrie would hear the roar of the rocket as it powered upwards from the launch pad and she would go to the window and watch the glow of the afterburners light up the whole sky and then gradually fade to a pale pink and disappear.

When Chet was away, Beth sometimes sat up late reading by the fireside. Before going upstairs, she would look in to see if Carrie was asleep and bend over and kiss her. But finding her cheeks wet, she would sigh and go silently from the room with a hand to her breast to soothe the pain in her heart.

One evening, Carrie's father returned home from a long flight. His co-pilot had been taken ill and he had had to stay at the controls for many extra hours. He was so tired that he did not eat his supper but went straight to bed.

At dusk, the sky grew very dark and the wind started to rise, and Carrie and her mother went around the house fastening the windows. 'I am worried about your father, Carrie,' her mother said as they finished supper. 'I have never seen him look so utterly drained. Be very quiet, my love, when you go to bed. I, too, am very tired. I will sleep upstairs in the spare room so that I shall not disturb him.'

Carrie's bedroom was downstairs next to the sitting room. She said her prayers and climbed into bed and lay awake listening to the rain pattering against the window panes and gurgling in the gutters. The thunder grew louder and the wind whistled in the chimneys, flinging itself against the walls of the house so that even the beams started to shake.

Lightning flickered around the walls of her room and then came a giant flash and a clap of thunder. She smelled smoke. She scrambled out of bed, threw on her dressing gown and tried the light switch. It did not work. With a beating heart, she opened her bedroom door.

Smoke was billowing around the house. The television set had exploded. Electricity sockets had been hurled across the room and flames were climbing the curtains and tracking across the carpet with extraordinary speed.

'Mother! Father!' she called, but her voice had no strength. *'Fire! Fire!'* she screamed but the sound she made was no more than a whimper. All those years of being quiet had taken away her voice.

Carrie ran up the stairs. *'Father!'* she cried. She tried to open the door of her parents' bedroom. It refused to budge. She put all her weight against it. The heat had warped its timbers and it still resisted her.

Behind her, in the hallway, a window blew out with a whoosh and the flames swept towards the stairs. She heaved at the door of the spare room and got it half open. Blinded by smoke and with her eyes streaming, she felt her way to her mother's bed. *'Mother! Mother! Wake up!'* Her mother made no movement.

Grabbing hold of Beth by her shoulders, she pulled her out of bed and dragged her out of the room to the landing. As they slid down the stairs, flames were already licking the lower steps. Sobbing and gasping with the exertion, she got her mother to the front door, slipped back the catch and pulled her outside.

The door slammed behind her. They were locked out. The rain hit them like water from a fire hose and within seconds they were soaked to the skin. Carrie pulled her mother into the shelter of the big tree. She took off her dressing gown and covered her. Beth's face was as white as paper but she was breathing.

There was a roar from the hall and sparks like fireflies swarmed from a gaping window. The stairs had fallen in. *'Father!'* she called again but the wind plucked the cry from her mouth and carried it away.

Tears of rage and despair joined the rain streaming down her face. The window of his bedroom seemed impossibly high up. Even if she could climb the big tree, she would never be able to reach it. The gap between them was too great. But she must climb it and warn him.

The branches of the cedar were threshing back and forth in the gale. Carrie scrambled onto the lowest. A sudden gust took her higher and she caught on to the branch above and with a strength she did not believe she possessed, pulled herself up. It happened again and again and in a miraculously short time she was level with the upper window.

But her strength was all spent. She had not felt the pain before, but now it came to her. Her feet were scorched, her arms were torn and her head was giddy with exhaustion. She was shivering so much that at any moment she felt she would lose her precarious hold on the branch and plunge to the ground.

She measured the distance to the window. She could never reach it. A wisp of smoke curled out of the top of it. Sheet lightning lit up the whole sky and the thunder rumbled like a roll of drums at an execution. 'Please help,' she whispered. 'Someone please help.'

There came a fluttering of wings in the branches above her. Startled, she looked up. *The nightingale!* Bursting into song, its entreaty seemed to soar heavenwards where the dark clouds were parting to allow a glimpse of the stars. *How could hope be dead and courage lost until this appeal was heard?*

Then despair returned. How could this frail creature with its futile carolling change anything? The thunder still rumbled in the distance. Death and destruction were leaving the field in triumph.

Cradled by the swaying bough, Carrie slipped in and out of consciousness. The crash of splintering wood and glass returned her to her senses. Her father, coughing and choking with the smoke, was using a chair to knock out the window. Now he was twisting his sheets into a rope ... slowly ... painfully slowly ... climbing onto the sill ... she must get down and help him...

'Father!' she shouted. *'Hold on! I'm coming!'* As she lowered herself, she scanned the branches for a sight of the nightingale but it had flown away.

The fire engines were able to save most of the house and the parts that were damaged were rebuilt. Chet was never going to be well enough to work as a pilot again so he decided to do what he had always wanted. He grew a few crops and kept some cows and his wife and daughter helped him. They were not as well off as before but they were much happier.

Carrie's voice recovered. Her friends came to play and the house was once more full of the sound of children's laughter. The birds returned to the garden and the flowers regained their bright colours. But they never saw the nightingale again.

The Property of a Gentleman

At the age of twenty-five, Giles Purford inherited the title, together with a large portfolio of freehold properties in central London. The income from the commercial and residential rents added up to several million pounds a year and he had no need to work. He lived in a large house in rural Surrey and indulged his taste for hunting, shooting and ocean racing. He was on the board of several charities and belonged to the local amateur dramatic society, occasionally appearing in undemanding roles.

One afternoon in January, he had finished tea and was stalking up and down the drawing room, his hands clasped behind his back, his face a picture of gloomy resignation. A hard frost had set in and there was no prospect of hunting for the next few days.

Other possible diversions were not available. The following day, his wife was lunching out and his farm manager was away at the livestock market. If his two sons had been at home, he would have taken them out and frightened a few pheasants but they had just returned to boarding school.

His wife, Joanna, watched him with feelings which were a mixture of affection and exasperation. 'Just for once, Giles, why don't you spend a day at your office?'

Her husband wrinkled his nose. 'What's the point? The managing agents handle all the rents. The office is tiny and it's run on a shoestring.'

'All the same, you are the chairman. The people who work there should sometimes see their boss. It would be good for their morale.'

'They see me when I turn up for board meetings.'

'That's only once a year. I bet you don't even know their names.'

Purford stooped to put a log on the fire. 'I certainly do. The manager is an admirable chap called Rees. Denise is the receptionist-cum-typist and there is, or should be, a clerk who does odd jobs and sorts out any complaints. He left a month ago. We have been looking for a replacement.'

'*For a month!* Doesn't that worry you?'

'It puzzles me.'

'Then go there tomorrow. You might find it stimulating.'

'Boring, more likely. I shall only see what Rees allows me to see.'

'Then go incognito. You know how much you love dressing up.'

Her husband smiled. 'Is that a serious suggestion?'

She laughed. 'Not really.'

He rubbed his chin. 'Well, I might take you up on it anyway.' Deep in thought, he walked slowly towards his study. The Labrador yawned and stretched but, seeing no hope of an outing, settled once more beside the hearth.

Purford picked up the telephone and put a call through to his office. He was a fair mimic and the voice that he carried in his head was that of the village postmaster, a man in his sixties. He was put through to Mr Rees. 'I'm ringing about your advertisement for a Complaints Clerk. I saw it in the evening paper.'

'Who am I speaking to?'

'Mr Brumby. John, to my friends. Have you filled the position?'

'We have had a lot of applicants. None of them were suitable.'

'May I come to your office for an interview?'

'Have you any experience of dealing with complaints?'

'No, but I catch on quickly.'

'What was your last job?'

'I haven't been employed for some time. To tell the truth, I have been trying to get fit.'

'Fit for what?'

'Fit for work, Mr Rees.'

'We have a young, go-ahead team here. I'm not sure that an older gentleman would be able to keep up.'

'Who said I was an older gentleman?'

'How old are you?'

'Young at heart, Mr Rees.'

'Very well, Mr Brumby, I am impressed with your keenness and I will spare you a few minutes. Be here tomorrow morning. Eight o'clock sharp and bring some references. Denise will tell you how to get here.' He switched the call to the receptionist.

Next morning, Purford was up before it was light. He spent an hour in a closet off his dressing room before emerging in a grey wig, drooping moustache and a worn pinstripe suit. He had given his chauffeur the day off and drove himself to the station. He travelled second class and then took a bus to Marble Arch and walked the rest of the way.

The office consisted of three rooms on the ground floor of an elegant corner house in a garden square. The first floor was used for board meetings and the upper floors had been converted into apartments for the use of company directors.

As Purford mounted the steps, a young woman opened the front door to sign for a delivery. She gave him a glossy vermilion smile. 'You must be Mr Brumby,' she said. 'Mr Rees is in his office. He is expecting you.'

Rees did not look up. He pointed to a chair and continued to leaf through the papers on his desk. At last he raised his head and squinted at his visitor through heavy horn-rimmed glasses. His sparse hair was oiled and combed forward to cover his baldness and a protruding upper lip was dressed with a toothbrush moustache.

'Ah, Mr Brumby,' he said. 'So you wish to work for a property company?'

'Yes, Mr Rees.' Purford spoke in a dry, husky voice. 'My old mother always used to say to me, "Mark my words, Son, you can't go wrong with bricks and mortar."'

'And did you follow your mother's advice?'

'My ambitions were boundless, Mr Rees, but I have been held back by lack of resources.'

Rees sniffed. 'You are not alone, Mr Brumby. You may take some comfort from that. Did you bring your references?'

'I looked at them, Mr Rees, but I decided that they were not a fair reflection of my ability.'

'So you left them behind?'

'To tell the truth, yes.' He curled the ends of his moustaches. 'But if I know my man, you set little store by the opinions of others. You have the insight and experience to trust your own judgement.'

'Insight cannot be taught,' said Mr Rees portentously. 'It is something a few of us are born with.'

Denise bustled in with a cup of coffee.

'No time for that.' Rees waved her away.

Denise stood her ground. 'Have a heart, Mr Rees. It's for Mr Brumby. He had no coat on when he arrived and it's ever such a cold morning.' She plonked the cup down on the table. 'There you are, dear. That will put roses in your cheeks.'

Rees cleared his throat noisily. 'Please return to your duties, Denise … and try to finish your breakfast before you come to work.'

'It's only a raspberry yoghurt, Mr Rees.' She wiped her mouth with the back of her hand, gave a little hitch to her miniskirt and went back to the front desk.

Rees sucked air through his teeth. 'I would be going out on a limb for you, Mr Brumby. I don't know what His Lordship would say if he knew that we were taking on people who showed up here without any references.'

'I'm greatly in your debt, Mr Rees. May I start at once?'

Rees waggled his head. 'I had hoped to give you a week's trial but I think it would be prudent to take each day at a time. In view of your age, your title will be that of Senior Complaints Executive.' He looked at his watch. 'You had better go to your desk straight away. Mrs Porter is due at any moment. Tell her that we can't help and get rid of her as soon as you can.'

Denise knocked on the door. 'Mrs Porter is here, Mr Rees.'

Mr Rees put out his head. 'Mr Brumby will see you today, Mrs Porter. Now, if you will excuse me–'

'*Just a moment, Mr Rees!* You tell that girl to behave more ladylike. Every time I walk through the door she is painting her nails or swinging her legs like a nightclub hostess. *It just ain't decent!*'

'Very well, Mrs Porter, I will have a word with her. Now, if you don't mind, I have some important business to attend to.' He shut the door firmly behind him.

Mrs Porter waddled into the general office. She was weighed down by two large shopping bags and her coat was covered in what looked like dog hair. A spaniel, grey in the muzzle and overweight, panted along behind her.

'Ooh,' she sighed. 'It is nice to take the weight off me feet. And Rover will be glad of a rest. He's not a young dog, not any more he ain't.' She looked around her. 'You must be very important, Mr Brumby, to have all this room to yourself.'

'I am a very junior member of the staff, Mrs Porter. In fact, I am the new boy. Now, how can I help you?'

Mrs Porter's cheeks turned pink with indignation. 'Do you mean to say that you haven't read my file?'

'I prefer to come to the problem with a fresh mind,' replied Mr Brumby.

'Ooh, you're a cool one and no mistake.' She peered at him through rheumy, red-lidded eyes. 'My Arthur – he's been dead this twelvemonth – he used to say if you have to tell a porkie, tell it with a plum.'

'Aplomb?'

'That's what I said.'

'Mrs Porter–'

'Mr Brumby. I have come about Rover. I have lost count of the number of times I have called to complain but nothing ever gets done. I have warned Mr Rees. If I have told him once, I have told him a hundred times. Mr Rees, I said, I will wear you down before you wear me down. Isn't that right, Rover?' She patted the dog's head.

'A very nice dog, Mrs Porter and, if I may say so, a very contented dog.'

She gaped at him. '*Contented!* Mr Brumby! A blind man could see that you know nothing about dogs. You are looking at a very unhappy dog. A dog with a grievance. A grievance which is growin' day by day against the 'ole of 'umanity!'

'What is troubling Rover, Mrs Porter?'

'That's more like it, Mr Brumby. Well, I will tell you. Rover likes a constitutional every evening, regular like. If he doesn't get it, he carries on something terrible, pining and whining until you think his heart is going to break.'

'I don't quite understand what that has got to do with–'

'If His Lordship heard about it, Mr Brumby, there would be a fine old rumpus, I can tell you. Heads would roll.'

'Is Lord Purford a dog lover?'

'Of course he is, like all the h'aristocracy. If he could see Rover of an evening, clambering up on the sofa, his poor old legs trembling with the effort, just to get a sight of something green. If he could see the way he tries to put his paws on the window sill so he can get a glimpse of the trees in the park.'

'Why can't you take Rover to the park, Mrs Porter?'

Mrs Porter struggled to find the words. 'I … I cannot believe I am hearing this, Mr Brumby. I live on the fifth floor and there isn't a lift. I am tired at the end of the day and my legs aren't what they should be … and I'm not far off seventy … now if I could have a flat on the ground floor…'

'I'm sure that can be arranged, Mrs Porter. The company has a wide range of accommodation and–'

'*Mr Brumby!*' Rees stomped out of his office. 'You will kindly refer to me before you offer improved terms to our tenants.' He helped Mrs Porter out of her chair. 'Alright, Mrs P, you have had your little moan. Now please leave us to get on with our work.'

'But what am I to do about Rover, Mr Rees?' She produced a grubby handkerchief from the recesses of her clothing and dabbed at her eyes.

'The trees in the park will be much better off without Rover's attentions. You will just have to persuade him to go for a walk in the morning.'

Mrs Porter wagged a finger furiously at him. 'Rover will never agree to that. He is like me – old and tired and set in his ways. Why did you have to interfere, you miserable old buzzard? Mr Brumby and I were getting on famously. All I am asking for is a ground-floor flat.'

'Which is out of the question, Mrs Porter. It is way beyond your means.' Rees urged her towards the door.

'Don't think you have got rid of me. *I will be back!*' Mrs Porter was still shaking her fist as she crossed the road.

Two other callers came in quick succession. Doris Dillchamber, a spinster of uncertain age, arrived to complain about Mr Chaunter, a neighbour, who was learning the guitar and had taken to serenading her at all hours of the day and night. She was followed by Mr Jencks protesting that Chirpy Charlie, his pet budgerigar, had not sung a note since Mrs Tench, who occupied the flat beneath them, had taken to walking up and down her balcony swinging a censer and reciting from the Song of Songs.

No sooner had the door closed on Mr Jencks than Brumby was summoned to Mr Rees's office. 'You are spending far too long with these tenants, Mr Brumby. Some of them just come here because it helps to pass the time. Don't encourage them.' He scowled at his watch. 'It is midday already and you haven't even looked at the written complaints.' He rustled a tray full of correspondence.

The doorbell rang and a few seconds later Denise tapped on the door. 'Miss Honeycomb to see Mr Brumby.'

'I have had my eye on that young lady,' said Mr Rees. 'Don't give her any more rope or she will hang us all with it.' He left the door slightly ajar and his eyes followed Miss Honeycomb as she sauntered in, her high heels click-clacking on the parquet floor.

She threw off a sable wrap to reveal a slinky cocktail dress. 'I'm afraid I didn't get much sleep last night,' she giggled.

Mr Brumby pulled out a chair for her.

'Where is the ogre?' she whispered.

'I'm not sure that I know what you mean.'

'Of course you know.' She gave him a huge wink and a piece of mascara landed on the top of the desk. 'What happened to Freddy?'

'Freddy?'

'Freddy Frickweld. The Complaints Clerk before you.'

'I believe he left.'

'I bet he got the sack. He was always larking about. He used to call Denise "The Knees" and as for Mr Rees–'

'Miss Honeycomb!'

'Please call me Henrietta,' she murmured.

'Very well, Henrietta. What is it that you came here to discuss?'

The girl's mouth drooped. 'You looked ever so fierce when you said that.' Then she beamed. 'But I know that behind that stern manner there beats a heart of gold. So, I am going to tell you everything just as if I was talking to my favourite uncle.'

'Are you sure that is wise?'

'Well I have always been a bit of a chancer, so here goes.' She took a deep breath. 'I rent one of your nicest flats. Daddy found it for me. He is very thick with Lord Purford. They shoot or sail together … one of the two. I wanted to buy my own flat but Daddy refused to advance the money.' She punished a lip with a pretty row of teeth. 'He said that I was wild and irresponsible and needed to grow up.'

Mr Brumby nodded. 'I'm sure your father wants to do only what is best for you.'

'But everyone in the house is so old and stuffy – not sweet and understanding like you, Mr Brumby.' She reached across the table and took his hands in hers. 'I admit that I sometimes come home very late … and I give parties … and I have lots of boyfriends … and, of course, they sometimes call round.' She gave a helpless shrug. 'After all, one is only young once…'

'Go on.' Brumby looked very stern.

'Well … to be completely honest …' Miss Honeycomb, feeling her cheeks growing warm, tossed her hair around her head, 'some of them aren't really boyfriends … I meet them in nightclubs … and it's awful saying good-bye … especially if you are having a good time … so I let them drive me home … and then they want to come in for a coffee … and one thing leads to another … do you see what I am trying to say, Mr Brumby?'

'Only too clearly, Henrietta, and, as you say, one thing leads to another. So, the tenants will get fed up with all the comings and goings and complain to the company. Then we will have to investigate and if we decide that the house is being used for immoral purposes, we shall not be able to let you stay.'

Miss Honeycomb's eyes filled with tears. 'It doesn't feel immoral, Mr Brumby, not at the time. Although I must admit I do get some quite nice presents.' She retrieved her hands and stroked the fur wrap. 'Mummy says that I should refuse to accept them but that seems so silly, After all, I am trying to save up for my own flat.'

Mr Brumby sighed. 'Henrietta, why did you come here today?'

'Because I know that there is going to be trouble,' she sniffled. 'It's such bad luck. All I need is another few months and I will have enough for the down payment.'

Mr Brumby rubbed his chin. It was a habit he had when he was thinking. 'Supposing,' he said at last, 'that the company was prepared to let you buy your flat?' Out of the corner of his eye, Brumby could see Mr Rees's door open a fraction. 'And supposing it agreed to accept whatever you could raise now to provide a deposit?' The door opened wider. 'What would you do in return?'

Miss Honeycomb's eyes became rounder and rounder and for a few moments she could not find the words. 'If the company did that for me, Mr Brumby,' she said at last, ' I would knock on the doors of all the people in the house and say that I was sorry and I would promise to be a model neighbour in future.' A single tear rolled down her cheek. She flicked it away with her hand. 'It would be hard, Mr Brumby, but I would keep my promise. Daddy might be cross when he found out but–'

'I don't think your father would be cross. I believe he would be proud of his daughter and I would be surprised if he did not feel that she deserved a little more help.'

An anguished moan like an animal in pain had been coming from Mr Rees's office and steadily growing in volume. Now the door was flung open and the manager flew out of his office like a stone released from a catapult.

'This interview is over,' he bellowed. 'Miss Honeycomb, please pay no attention to Mr Brumby. To listen to him you might think that he owned the company. Mr Brumby, please draw half a day's wages and travel expenses on your way out. I don't know where you came from but please go back there.'

***

'You are back very early, Darling,' said Joanna Purford when her husband came through the door. She dodged his kiss. 'No! Not till those awful whiskers go!'

He laughed. 'What a day! Or rather, half a day. *I got fired!*'

'Serve you right for sailing under false colours!'

'I am rather ashamed of myself but I will feel better about it when I make one or two changes. First of all, Mr Rees and Denise must have an increase in salary. You would not believe what they have to put up with.' As he mounted the stairs to his dressing room, his mind turned to the problems of Miss Honeycomb and Mrs Porter's dog. While he soaked in the bath, he planned several more good deeds.

The Best Man

Robey had a way with him. There was no mistaking it. We were new boys together and I saw it that very first day at school. There was this small, golden-haired creature leaping up and down the stairs exhorting, threatening, cajoling poor old Jim the handyman, who lumbered behind him bowed down under the weight of an enormous trunk. By the time the pair had reached the tiny attic room under the roof, Jim was so helpless with laughter and so breathless from his exertions that it was as much as Robey could do to persuade him to take five shillings for labour worth double or more.

Everything that Robey did was done with style. He didn't work very hard but his indolence had that touch of artistry which compelled reluctant admiration and his teachers seemed almost grateful for a fraction of the industry demanded of their more assiduous pupils.

To games he brought the same panache. Some of the boys took up cricket; others rowed. Robey contrived to do both. He treated good and bad bowling alike. The subtleties of spin, the honest brutality of pace were greeted with the same vigorous flailing action which might see his wicket broken or the ball hoisted over the tops of the chestnut trees and out of the ground. His innings was usually short and glorious. I, who received coaching during the holidays, would spend twice as long at the crease in the accumulation of half as many runs. It was Robey's performance, not mine, that was remembered.

When it was hot, he would abandon the playing fields, scratch his name from the team list on the house notice board and append a note, 'Sorry – gone to the river.' Independence of mind in a junior boy is little encouraged by those in authority. Discipline and conformity are two sides of the same bright and shining coin and he did not escape the inevitable sanctions.

As he became taller and heavier, Robey developed into a powerful oarsman, if not a very elegant one. It was rare that he returned to the boathouse without some adventure to recount and the long summer evenings would find him in the nearby tavern, a tankard of cider in his hand, making as much of a passage between Windsor Bridge and Cuckoo Weir as a sailor might a single-handed rounding of the Horn.

I was jealous of Robey from the start. He was the sun, the rest of us mere planets drawn irresistibly into his orbit. To withdraw from his influence was to see one's life fall into shadow. But what to do? I could neither embrace his friendship nor disown his company. The dilemma became an obsession with me. It affected my work, soured my days. Only with difficulty did I succeed in dissembling my feelings.

But I must remain calm, I told myself. All this would soon change. School days were nearly over. The stern business of earning a living was about to begin. Robey would find himself at a great disadvantage compared with most of his contemporaries. His parents were not well off. They had struggled to pay the school fees and could not afford to send him to university. He could not look to them for assistance.

Robey had been taken on by a firm of insurance brokers but he was not sanguine about his prospects. 'I have few brains, no money and hardly a connection worth the mention. It will mean starting at the bottom.'

'You will prosper, Robey. I feel sure of it,' I replied. Weasel words.

'Very slowly,' he said glumly. 'But for you things will be different. First, university and then a job in your father's property company. In five years' time I shall still be a junior clerk. You will have a directorship. You will be miles ahead of me – out of sight.'

I couldn't disagree. It was a prospect I anticipated with relish. Life was like a great ocean. I would bounce along on top of the waves while Robey, encumbered by his diving gear, trudged through the silt on the sea bed. Every now and then I would give him a tug on the rope to show that he might be allowed up on deck for a brief word of encouragement or commiseration.

'We must keep in touch, Robey,' I said.

'Oh, yes,' he echoed, 'we must. I shall always think of you as my best friend.'

That autumn I went up to university. Like many before me, I ran up accounts with the wine merchants and tailors and with other tradesmen in the town and, in due course, applied to my father to assist in settling them. I gave small parties for selected friends in my rooms in the expectation that they would become a byword for wit and brilliance. If they were something less, the outlay expended on such diversions far exceeded my estimation.

None of this would have mattered had Robey languished in his sunless office in Cheapside doomed to permanent drudgery, to a life of processing claims, quoting premiums and preparing dreary computations for uncongenial people. Imagine then my consternation when I discovered that he was having fun. And more fun than was seemly in a young man of little means and few prospects. Week after week, there he was in the society magazines – at parties for this, parties for that, May balls, hunt balls, Ascot, Wimbledon, Goodwood, a glass of bubbly in his hand, a ravishing girl at his side and always wearing that expression of dazed exhilaration as if at any moment this run of undeserved good fortune must come to an end.

How was this conjuring trick performed? He had no decent clothes. There was that battered old dinner jacket that looked as if it had been picked up at a jumble sale. His shirts, I swear, were those nylon abominations that can be hung over the bath to drip dry. Minute examination of the pictures in the society magazines excited the suspicion that he turned his cuffs inside out to prolong their dishonourable existence by one more day. By rights the hostesses should have struck him off their lists. Run him out of town.

For some weeks I was quite cast down but I reminded myself that my finals were approaching. A thriving career in the business world beckoned. It would set me on the escalator while poor Robey would be left clambering step by painful step up from the basement.

I left university with a respectable degree and devoted a month to leisure and travel, journeying in some considerable style through countries still unvisited by the spoiling hand of prosperity. Few things are more reassuring to the Western eye than a brief acquaintance with places where time has stood still and the conditions of the people have changed little since the Middle Ages. I returned with a fresh perspective, my anxieties about Robey somewhat assuaged.

It was midsummer and halfway through Henley Week. I had just taken up my sinecure in my father's business. The salary was generous and the work undemanding. It was time to make a fresh assessment of my rival's situation.

I telephoned Robey. Could he join my father's party the following day? Lunch in the Leander tent. Smoked salmon and lobster washed down by vintage Krug. Superb cheeses. Tropical fruit flown in from a Pacific island. We were entertaining important businessmen but my father had suggested that I might like to invite a friend.

'I'm sorry, old man, but I can't,' he began. My heart soared. Poor old Robey couldn't get away from the office. The weather was roasting and he was stuck at his desk.

'I'm taking a small party myself,' he said. My spirits plummeted. Houdini had struggled free of his chains again.

'Nothing like your bash,' he went on, 'just a picnic ... wine from Sainsbury's ... strawberries from Marks ... a few soppy girls...'

I knew then that he had spoiled the day for me and so it proved. A faint hope remained that I might spot Robey's ancient Sunbeam wedged in among the Bentleys in the car park, his disconsolate guests rooting about in the boot for warm drumsticks or coronation chicken. But no. There they were in a picked spot on the edge of the river, sprawled on rugs in the dappled shade of a willow tree. Robey and his chums were attired in old boaters and blazers that looked as if they had been borrowed from the local repertory company, the girls exquisite in white cotton dresses and large picture hats, hampers brimming with goodies, bottles suspended from fishing rods cooling in the water.

All through a dull lunch devoted to a discussion of the merits or otherwise of building a hypermarket on the Slough trading estate, I could hear their laughter. The woman next to me kept turning in their direction and saying, 'Someone's having fun.' I think that, at that moment, I really hated Robey.

It was after three before I could get away and stroll down to the water. I had drunk too much and felt unwell and was in a poor humour. A young woman left her companions as I approached. She waved a thermos. 'Do you feel as awful as you look?' she asked.

'Worse,' I told her.

'What you need is strong black coffee and lots of sympathy.' She had a trim figure, hair like dark flame and green eyes that crinkled when she smiled.

Robey came up and introduced us. This was Elsa. I could tell that he was in love with her. The trouble was that by that time, I was too.

We both saw a great deal of Elsa over the next few years. She refused to talk about marriage. 'We are all still so young and I have more important things to think about.' But there was this understanding, nevertheless, that she would marry one or other of us.

Time was on my side. Robey was still sharing a dreary flat in Battersea with friends. Still driving the old Sunbeam. He was not well paid and now that he was trying to save money, his social life was as flat as last week's lemonade. His circumstances and mine bore no comparison. I had recently put the money down on a small house in Fulham and celebrated my new directorship by purchasing a smart red Morgan sports car.

Elsa worked long hours as a nurse in a West London hospital and lived alone in a small rented flat in Hammersmith. Was she not lonely, I asked her?

'I did try sharing but my friends got so fed up with me coming home in the early hours of the morning and waking them all up that this seemed the only answer.' Elsa was pure gold, through and through.

She had tried to make the flat attractive but it was old-fashioned and gloomy. Even in summer it was as if the daylight was too exhausted by the time it had reached the bottom of the steps to penetrate into the bed-sitting room with its small window giving onto the area.

It was difficult to see Elsa during the week but she was always off at noon on Saturday, and Robey and I alternated in taking her out on the half day. One Sunday a month she would arrange an excursion and the three of us would go out together, perhaps down the river to Greenwich or, in the summer, picnic in one of the parks.

Over a period, the tradition evolved that when the Saturday came around, whoever's turn it was to see Elsa would bring her a present. Robey always told me what he intended to give her and very often asked my advice. *My advice!* How little he understood how I felt about him. *What an imbecile to play into my hands!*

I might suggest that he arrive with an assortment of chocolates greatly favoured by the undiscriminating. The next week I would turn up with a gift-wrapped box of violet creams from Charbonnel & Walker. On another occasion he showed me with great pride a shawl that he had purchased at the Chelsea Crafts Fair. Commonplace I thought it. I bought her a lovely scarf from Hermès.

Elsa protested. 'You must stop giving me these presents. Neither of you can afford it.'

I could afford it very comfortably I told her. I assured her that it placed her under no obligation. It gave me pleasure. In this way, gradually, persistently, I set about undermining my rival. Robey seemed quite oblivious to the danger. The fool suspected nothing, evinced not the smallest resentment. On the contrary, he expressed delight that Elsa should receive tributes worthy of her, lamenting only that circumstances prevented him from doing as much.

It was a cold winter. By late November the birds had robbed the holly trees of berries. At Christmas there was a heavy snowfall. In March, the Serpentine froze.

Elsa became ill and was confined to her bed. She felt sick and feverish. The doctor thought she might have a touch of 'flu. Otherwise he could find little wrong with her beyond overwork. Keep warm was his advice. And try to get some rest. If possible, take a holiday when the weather got warmer.

Robey telephoned me at my office. 'I'm seeing Elsa this evening,' he said. 'What do you think I should take her?'

'Bring her some flowers.'

'I brought her some nice daffodils yesterday.'

'She gets these shivery spells. She might like some ginger wine. It would warm her up.'

'What a genius you are,' Robey enthused. 'Why didn't I think of that?'

The following morning was a Saturday. I arrived at noon with a bottle of champagne.

'What you need, Elsa, is a pick-me-up.' I pointed a disparaging finger at the ginger wine. 'I sometimes wonder whether Robey really cares for you when I see the things he gives you.'

'Oh, don't say that,' Elsa protested. 'Please don't say that.'

She sat up and pulled the blankets around her shoulders. We toasted each other a little sombrely for she looked very pale, her cheekbones very prominent in the thin face.

'How do you feel, Elsa? Are you eating properly?'

'I only seem to be able to pick at my food. Then I get this awful nausea...' she sipped at her drink and smiled bravely. 'But this will do me good.'

I placed my glass on the bedside table, pushing the flowers to one side.

Elsa frowned. 'Please leave them.' She stretched out a hand and nudged the vase back into place.

'They are almost dead,' I said roughly.

'I know, but Robey went to such trouble to get them and they were probably very expensive. With weather like this they have to fly them in from places like the Scilly Isles.'

I took her hand. 'You can't go on like this, Elsa. Living in this place ... it's damp and poorly lit...'

'I'm fond of it. I know it isn't very grand but with the curtains drawn and the window shut it gets quite cosy...'

'I don't just mean this flat. You need someone who has resources ... someone in a position to look after you.

Don't you think it is time that we had a talk about us?
About the future? You know how much I–'

'Not now. Please not now.' She squeezed my hand
gently. 'Another time. When I am a little better.' She
closed her eyes and with a little sigh, sank back upon
the pillow.

I said nothing but I was tired of prevarication. A
short, sharp campaign was what I planned. Elsa could
not fail to be anxious about herself. Her resistance
would be low. Her illness had provided me with the
opportunity that I needed. In my mind I marshalled my
arguments. She had few savings. Her parents were
struggling to cope with a hill farm in the Scottish
borders. They had nothing to spare. Nursing was the
only training that she had but the work was very
demanding. It was now affecting her health. She needed
a new life. I could offer it.

A few days of gentle but persistent pressure and
she would submit. Within a month we could be
engaged. And married in the summer. As for Robey, the
sight of his face when he learned that the man he
regarded as a trusted friend had robbed him of what lay
closest to his heart, that would make up for everything.

I kissed her. 'We will talk about it again the next
time I see you,' I said firmly. 'Meanwhile I want you to
think about what I have said.'

On the way home I called at Moyses Stevens and
ordered a large bunch of superb red tulips. I had them
sent straight round to Elsa's flat. I would leave her alone
until Monday, I decided. The tulips' silent advocacy
was worth half a day of blandishment. By Monday
evening, I promised myself, I should find her ready to
listen to me.

I learned afterwards what happened from Robey. He went to see Elsa a little after noon the next day, a Sunday. He descended the steps to the area, tapped on the door and then on her window but received no answer. Better to let her sleep, he thought. She had looked so pale and washed out, she needed the rest. He was just going back up the steps when something made him turn back. The curtains across the window were half drawn. He could just see the edge of her bedhead and the bedside table. And my tulips.

'They were drooping. Ready to be thrown out. I was astonished. I know you would never buy anything but the very best.'

'Never!' My heart stood still. What was coming?

Robey had smashed the window, got in and dragged Elsa to the air. Her lips were blue. She was unconscious. When the ambulance came he sat inside with her on the way to the hospital. It was a very close call the doctor said. An hour later ... well, it didn't bear thinking about.

'We get lots of these problems,' the heating engineer said. He was tinkering around in a cupboard in the tiny galley kitchen that adjoined Elsa's bedroom. 'Old boilers with faulty flues. Especially in a bad winter. And the trouble with North Sea Gas is that you can't smell it. It's lethal. Take my word for it.' He shuffled through the pockets of his overall. 'The only answer is regular maintenance ... I have a contract with me here somewhere...' He replaced a few parts and left the old ones on the kitchen table.

Robey asked me to be his best man when Elsa and he got married in the summer. In duty bound, I felt that I had to drag him off to Moss Brothers and hire him a morning suit. I even lent him a shirt. The church was in the middle of nowhere. Nothing but moor and mountains and an enormous sky. Very romantic if you were in the mood for it. The place was packed. It took Robey ten minutes to walk past the pews with all those girls making sheep's eyes at him and wanting a last word before he was finally lost to them. He still had a hole in the sole of a shoe but I didn't tell him. There were limits to what I was prepared to do for him.

It was an odd feeling standing shoulder to shoulder with him, waiting for Elsa to come down the aisle. Rubbing the wedding ring nervously between finger and thumb, half hoping that I could summon a genie who would etherise Robey in a puff of smoke and leave me to carry off the bride in triumph.

I wasn't sure that I could bring myself to give the ring to Robey when the moment came. To watch him slide it on Elsa's finger. To watch them kiss shyly and pledge eternal love. It was almost unendurable. Had Robey meant it kindly when he asked me to be his best man or had he taken all this time to revenge himself by putting me through this ordeal? Whatever I had done, nobody had the right to inflict this amount of suffering.

I was debating what would happen if I refused to part with the ring. There would be a scene. The wedding would probably have to be postponed. Given a breathing space, I might yet succeed in persuading Elsa that she was marrying the wrong man.

But I never got the chance. Robey had his own ring with him. A thin metal circlip from the boiler that the fitter had left behind. He had polished it up. That was what he slipped on Elsa's finger. And she is still wearing it.

People still talk about that wedding. If I see them coming down the street, I cross over to avoid them because I know exactly what they are going to say. 'Weren't you the best man at Robey's wedding? I'll remember that moment as long as I live. Your expression! *If you could have seen it!* By the way, have you still got the other ring?' I told you Robey had a way with him.

Coincidence

We were attending one of those conferences where doctors gather to discuss affairs of mutual concern and usually stay up late into the night talking and drinking too much. I do not remember who raised the subject of coincidence but it prompted one my companions to refill his glass, settle back in his chair and tell us of one particular instance which he thought might interest us.

'The woman – let us call her Emma, was a patient of mine,' he began. 'She was married to … Keith, a musician who played in a well-known orchestra. They had not been married very long when he was diagnosed with a progressive wasting disease. It was hereditary but it seemed to have lain dormant for a generation before re-emerging. There was no cure and no question, they were told, of having children.

'You can imagine their distress and disappointment but they tried to make the best of it. Keith had his music. Emma had a job in a primary school and she threw herself into her teaching. But it was not enough. Their marriage was crumbling.

'Keith begged her to leave him. At times, when she was close to despair, she almost persuaded herself that he meant it. But she loved him and he needed her. She could not abandon him. So they came to an agreement. She would stay but she could have a child by another man. It was understood between them that the man would be a stranger and that when he had played his part, he would vanish from their lives. Keith trusted her to bring this about. How she did it was up to her. He did not want to be told.

'Emma pursued all sorts of stratagems in her quest for a lover who was likely to fulfil these rather unusual conditions. Eventually, on a hot summer's afternoon in the Lake District, instinct persuaded her that, at last, she had found him. The man was already in a boat and so she hired one too and rowed over to a small island where willow trees provided shade from the sun and prying eyes.

'She was wearing a straw hat and a printed frock with cherries on it and carried a picnic basket. The man rested on his oars and allowed his boat to drift to the bank where she was laying out a large rug. He was tall, fair and heavily tanned and wearing an open-necked shirt and slacks. She opened a bottle of champagne and shared with him a light but delicious lunch of gulls eggs, cold chicken, raspberries and cream.

'She did most of the talking. She spoke softly and earnestly and he smiled and nodded his head. Then he undressed her and made love to her. Afterwards, he lit a cigarette and before she could stop him he started to tell her about himself. His name was Niels Vreden and he had a son called Frans. Alarmed, she broke in. Had he forgotten already the bargain that they had made?

'At least, he protested, she should tell him who she was. She shook her head. There was no need for him to know, for they must never meet again. He was hurt and angry, and said some things that made her cry.

'From this encounter, Emma gave birth to a daughter and they called her Julie. Eighteen years passed and Julie grew up to be a beautiful young woman. When Keith could no longer work, the family moved to a village in the West Country and rented a small house down by the harbour.

'Emma gave up her teaching job to look after him but his condition deteriorated quickly and he had to be moved into hospital. Julie and Keith, the man she believed to be her father, had always been very close. It frightened him to think that this might change if she discovered the exact nature of his illness. You may think that his fears were irrational but he was a very sick man. At his insistence, the truth was kept from the girl.

'It was no secret, however, that Keith was dying. Julie visited him whenever she could, often sitting at his bedside for hours on end. One day she came to see him accompanied by a boyfriend. As they emerged from the ward, a junior doctor who had only recently joined the staff gave her a sharp look, took her aside and asked her whether she had been given the full details of her father's illness.

'He cut short her reply. Plainly, she was ignorant of what was wrong with him. It was his painful duty, he told her, to dispel any illusions she might have. The disease – he went into some detail – was hereditary. Even if she escaped it, she was a carrier. If she married, she must remain childless. As a responsible person, she must see that there was no other option.

'He wanted her to stay and take some tests but her mind was in such turmoil that she fled from him. She had plans to go to university but she withdrew her application, took a job with a children's charity, moved out of her home and into lodgings.

'Julie became alienated from her mother. She felt that she should have trusted her with the truth about Keith's illness instead of hiding it from her all those years. She became a lonely and reclusive creature, withdrawing into herself, seeing little of her friends and seemed only to shake off her sorrows when she was out in the bay in her sailing boat.

'Her mother was alarmed by the change in her and begged her husband to let her tell Julie about her real father. But Keith was failing fast and had been moved to a hospice. He could not bear, he told her, to add to Julie's unhappiness. The girl was in no state to withstand another revelation. Nor could he endure losing her. Her devotion meant so much to him and he had only a few weeks left. He implored Emma not to tell her. Not until he died. Then she could tell her the truth.

'Keith died a fortnight later. The day after his funeral, Emma came to Julie's lodgings. They were both in a very emotional state. Emma wanted to be reconciled to her daughter. She wanted to tell her that she blamed herself for not speaking to her earlier about the difficulties that she and Keith had encountered in the early years of their marriage and try to explain why they had acted as they had.

'It seemed easier to talk about these things while they walked together and they set out on a path that rose steeply from the edge of the town and then ran along the top of the cliffs. Heavy rain during the night had given way to fitful sunshine and a bullying wind that shook the gorse bushes beside the muddy track. There came a rumble like thunder and the ground trembled beneath their feet.

'From far below, there came a cry borne to them on the wind. Julie pushed her way through the gorse before her mother could stop her and was clinging to a sapling on the very edge of the cliff. There had been a landslip, the second in the course of a month.

'Julie could see the figure of a man running across a small area of shingle to a rocky outcrop on the edge of the water. He was cut off and the tide was coming in fast. The two women ran down the hill and hurried through the narrow, cobbled lanes to the little port. There was no immediate help to be had. The fishing boats were all out at sea. A launch, skippered by one of the town's habitual drunkards would not start.

'In a ships' chandlers, they fretted while a call was put through to the coastguards. It was clear that by the time help arrived, it might be too late. They would have to take Julie's little boat. Mother and daughter clambered down a rusty iron ladder, started the auxiliary diesel and cast off. Beyond the harbour wall, the sea was choppy and the wind was stiffening every moment.

'They were no more than a hundred yards from the marooned man when the engine puttered to a stop. A wall of water caught the boat beam on and turned it over. Julie swam out from underneath, gasping for air, and clung to the keel. Through the spray, she caught a glimpse of the man. The rock on which he was standing was almost submerged and waves were breaking over his knees. She looked for her mother. There was no sign of her.'

Our companion stretched his long legs and drained his glass before continuing. 'I was a young specialist working in the general hospital at the time. All three were rescued but when Julie's mother was admitted, she was in a coma. I was put in charge of her case. I wondered whether she would ever regain consciousness. If she did, I was concerned that she might have suffered brain damage.

'Julie came to see her mother every day. I tried to get her to talk but she would say only a few words before relapsing into silence. It was painful to see so young and attractive a person in the grip of such depression.

'One day I took a telephone call from the young man who had been rescued with them. He wanted to meet Julie, he told me, but she was avoiding him. I taxed Julie with this. It was unkind of her, I said. She should let him come. It would be company for her.

'Julie had her mother's looks, her dark hair and high colouring. Her eyes flashed and for a moment I feared she would raise her hands to me. She did not want company, she cried. All she wanted was to be left alone. Then she sank back into that gloom that I had come to know so well.

'It soon became obvious that the young man was no quitter. I had tried to help him but without success. Then, a few days later, I had just drawn the curtains of Emma's cubicle after an examination when Julie and the young man came into the ward. I asked the chap to wait outside.

'Julie's eyes were red but I sensed that something extraordinary had changed. You could see it in the set of her head, in the swing of her body as she turned to watch him leave the room. In the past weeks, she had been like a ship becalmed. Now the wind was filling her sails.

'I told her that her mother had opened her eyes. She was going to recover. Julie gave a sort of gasping cry and would have run in to see her had I not restrained her. She would find her mother very tired and rather confused, I said. She must try to keep calm and spend no more than a few minutes with her.

' *"How can I stay calm?"* She waved a letter and pushed past me. I cannot bear to listen to women crying even when happiness is the cause of their tears and I did not linger.

'I got to know Emma fairly well over the next few weeks. She slowly recovered her strength and her mind became clearer. She talked about her husband, his illness, the impossibility of having children by him and the expedients to which she had been driven. Her frankness surprised me but, on reflection, I think that it was her way of retrieving events in her life which she feared might have been wiped from her memory during her period of unconsciousness.

'That day on the cliff path she had been on the point of telling Julie what had for so long been kept from her. Any relief she might have felt at lifting one shadow from her daughter's life was tempered by her anxiety at ushering in another. How was she to respond to the inevitable questions about Julie's real father? Who was he? What was he like? Where did he live? Had he got a family of his own? Could she meet him?

'But Keith had taken one of these burdens upon his own shoulders. He had left a letter for Julie with his solicitors, to be opened after his death. A wonderful letter, by all accounts, full of affection and tenderness. Julie read it again and again until it was creased and stained with her tears.

'Soon Emma was able to walk short distances unaided. She had, until then, pushed the accident to the back of her mind. It was a sign of her increasing confidence in making a full recovery that she wanted to find out exactly what had happened. When she was told that Julie's new boyfriend was the chap who had swum out to the boat, she wanted to meet him.

'I had been worried about Emma becoming overtired and I made the two promise that if they were allowed to visit together, they would not stay long. The boy was tall and slim and, I judged, in his late twenties. His tanned face spoke of a life lived in a warmer climate than could have been gained by visits to our own island.

'Seeing them together made an extraordinary impression on me. Here were two young people who had only met a few days earlier and yet the ease, the familiarity between them was most remarkable. It was as if they had known each other all their lives. The fates, I concluded, had done their best to keep them apart but had finally surrendered.

'The following afternoon, when I made my rounds, I left Emma with a clipping from the local newspaper. She would find out that the young man was an archaeologist who lived in Kenya. He had been visiting England when he read about the first landslip and hurried down to the West Country to hunt for fossils in the newly exposed section of cliff.

'When the boat capsized, he swam out to it. Julie was diving underneath it in increasingly desperate efforts to find her mother. By the time they reached Emma, she was unconscious but together they managed to bring her to the surface and support her until help arrived.

'There was a grainy photograph of someone being winched from the water by the crew of a helicopter.

The article added a few lines by way of background.
The young man's parents ran a safari business based in
Kenya but they had been killed a few years earlier
while flying in a small plane in the Masai Mara.

 'On my way out, the ward sister told me that Julie
and her friend, a Mr Frans Vreden, were in the waiting
room. I was about to tell her that I had given permission
for the two to visit Emma when I heard a commotion
behind me. She had collapsed. All the signs pointed to a
heart attack.'

The narrator folded his arms and looked around his
small audience. My neighbour scratched his head.
'Aren't you going to tell us what happened?'

'Emma made a full recovery.'

'I'm sure we are all pleased for her,' I said, 'but
what we all want to know is whether Julie was told the
truth. You could not let her marry her half-brother!'

The figure in front of the fireplace raised a pair of
heavy eyebrows by way of answer.

'Why won't you tell us?' we roared.

He put a finger to his lips. 'I promised to tell you
about a coincidence,' he said. 'Not about the laws of
consanguinity.'

We could cheerfully have murdered him.

Today of all Days

Ruth knew that she ought to have put that conversation out of her head. Forgot all that the policeman had said. Expunged from her mind the possibility that he might write to her. For what was the point? Alan was dead. Ash piled upon ash piled upon ash. And yet, underneath, the embers warmed her still. Proof that despite everything, that part of her still lived.

The sound of the mail van receded and with a show of casualness, Richard finished his second cup of coffee, rose from the breakfast table and stalked across the hall. She knew exactly how long he took to sort his letters from hers. The knowledge irritated her no more and no less than the other little ceremonies in Richard's day which over the years had achieved the status of ritual. That he took a few seconds longer than usual must mean that a letter had arrived for her with an intriguing postmark or addressed in a hand unknown to him. She waited until the investigation was completed and she heard the door of her husband's study close behind him. Then, for some reason for which she was not prepared to account to herself, she shuffled off her shoes, tiptoed to the post table, picked up the small package in its padded brown envelope and turned it over. Richard must have examined it and left it face down. An absurd subterfuge but wonderfully in character. He wouldn't question her straight away but leave it a day or two before enquiring whether she had heard from her sister Deborah, knowing perfectly well, of course, that the letter had not come from her.

Leaving a marker buoy over the spot so that he could send his divers down later.

Deborah was married to a Spanish businessman and lived in Madrid. Every year she went to stay with her for a few days in May so that she could be there on the twentieth. Richard could hardly have forgotten that date but Alan's name was never mentioned between them. Richard's memory was like a far-off country for which very few visas were issued.

She put the envelope in her pocket, leaving her other letters on the table. Slipping quietly past the study, she hurried upstairs to her bedroom and pushed the package to the back of the drawer of the dressing-room table. As she raised her head she started at her face in the mirror. She looked furtive, as if she had been detected in some action which she wished to keep concealed.

Moving to the window, she gazed down into the garden. The church fête was being held that afternoon and Richard had agreed to open it and say a few words. Preparations were in full swing. Trestle tables were being set out on the lawn. A workman was threading cable through the branches of the cherry trees for the public address system. A van was arriving with props for the Punch and Judy show. If her son David had lived, he would be there with the other children, running races, riding on the shaggy Dartmoor pony or sprawled on the grass watching the conjuror.

But David had drowned. He was only two. They had been together in the garden. Something had told her that she shouldn't answer the telephone. But she had left him. She couldn't have been away for more than a minute or so. David could not have crossed the expanse of lawn in the time unless he had sprouted wings. When she found him he was lying on the bottom of the swimming pool, staring up at her. She would never forget those astonishing violet eyes. Wide open as if he had to absorb, take in, remember everything in those last few seconds before his future was removed from him.

Perhaps if they had had another child, things would have been different, but David's death had been an earthquake. It had thrown up a mountain range between Richard and her. To cross that barrier took more faith, more strength, more commitment than they had been able to find.

Life has to go on. In a forgotten corner of the world riven by tribal warfare it was just one more tragedy among so many. There was only so much help and sympathy to go around. They could hardly behave as if the grief of a middle-ranking diplomat and his wife was some sort of hard currency which could be exchanged for preferential treatment. Work had seemed the only solution. To submerge her misery in the sheer exhaustion of getting through each day.

She was a trained nurse. She offered her services to the UN team in one of the distribution camps set up to cope with the refugee problem. There had been opposition from Richard and from some of his colleagues. Hints that the wife of a diplomat should not be seen working at the coal face. Her role was to be at Richard's side wearing a bright smile and a pretty cotton frock. But she had ignored them. There was a job to be done and she could do it. Had she known that she would meet Alan, she might have been more circumspect.

Alan Dacre was a foreign correspondent with one of the nationals. He was on his way from somewhere to somewhere else and had attached himself to the camp for a few days. He seemed content to make himself useful doing odd jobs around the place before moving on. Very different from the image that had preceded him of wine, women and, well, war. He managed things so that he was never very far from where she was working; like a stray dog intent on finding someone to adopt it. That someone wasn't going to be her, she told herself. She was proof against the weather-beaten good looks, the ragged bush shirt, the desert boots – and the reputation that came with them. More than proof, armour-plated.

At the end of each day they would have a drink together and she would unwind a little. She didn't ask him about his job or where he had been and what he had seen. It showed in his eyes. She hadn't been prepared for that or for his weariness. For Alan was deathly tired. Tired in his head and in his heart. He was like a seabird on a long ocean crossing. He had got close to the end of himself. What she had done wasn't important. She was just a small boat that happened to be in the right place at the time. Somewhere to perch until he was strong enough to resume his journey.

At first she persuaded herself that it was all part and parcel of the work she was doing, but self-deception had never been one of her strong points and she had been relieved that Richard's new posting had come through a few days later. They were being sent to Madrid. A good posting. Was it ungenerous in her to feel that it had not been fully earned, that it owed something to sympathy for their recent bereavement?

There had been encouraging words from on high. It would mean promotion, new surroundings and a new challenge. But, reading between the lines, she was in no doubt that the mandarins in King Charles Street would be watching them carefully.

She went to Richard's dressing room and made his bed before going downstairs to clear away the breakfast things. There was her note on the kitchen table to remind her to look out a bottle of wine for the tombola. Inevitably Richard would miss it later and she would be scolded for choosing the wrong year. 'The Chiroubles needs drinking, Ruth. Why didn't you ask me first?' Another man would have told her off for not buying a bottle of plonk from the supermarket.

At exactly eleven o'clock she made a cup of coffee for her husband and carried it into the study. Richard was speaking into the hand-held microphone. The dictating machine was the fruit of one of her small rebellions. She didn't object to typing his letters but she wasn't prepared to sit on the edge of her chair with a notebook on her lap taking shorthand.

He frowned as if impatient of the interruption and paused to allow her to put down the tray on the corner of the desk. She kissed him on the forehead and left the room, closing the door softly behind her.

Richard was still a good-looking man. Tall and spare and blue-eyed, with the silvery hair and the long, narrow head, he might have passed for the archetype of the successful retired diplomat, but the eyes had lost their sharp focus and his face had the soft, puffy look of a fallen apple, the skin bruised as if by misfortune or disappointment. His appointment as First Secretary in Madrid had been the high-water mark. After that it was downhill all the way. Second-grade postings in South America. Late nights composing over-long reports that nobody bothered to read. Finally a desk job in London. Then retirement to Devonshire. Richard had suffered but not alone. In his civilised English way he had made sure that she had borne her share.

In the larder there were some cakes that she had made. She wrapped these in cling film and carried them out to one of the tables on the lawn. On her return journey she was waylaid.

'Mrs Gage, you said that we might have some small pot plants from the conservatory.'

Ruth clapped a hand to her head, 'And I had forgotten all about them. Let me help you with them. The geraniums are rather gaudy but the trailing lobelia is very pretty.'

Alan would chuckle if he could see her now, in her cashmere jumper and tweed skirt playing the lady of the manor. Would he find her so very much changed? Her figure was little altered, her dark hair still defying the grey.

She would walk him around the garden so that they could poke fun at everything. At the house with its garish orange brickwork and hideous Victorian gables, the front door with its William Morris stained glass. The preposterous standard roses that lined the path to the French windows, between whose ranks Richard would progress as if he was inspecting a guard of honour. The lily pond with its lugubrious carp, the driveway squeezed between the dark, overgrown rhododendrons. The pretentious stone pillars at the end that Richard had wanted to surmount with a pair of wild boar. These had proved beyond their means and they had settled for a rabbit and a squirrel instead.

Ruth returned to the house to find her husband rapping on the glass of the barometer.

'I hope the rain holds off. It's an awkward sort of day. Difficult to know what to wear.'

'I assumed that you would wear your white linen suit.' He would wear it even if it was snowing. 'You can always put on a pullover beneath your jacket.'

'I would rather not. It spoils the line of the coat.' He shuffled through the cards in his hand on which he had written some notes.

Ruth felt that something more was required of her. 'How is the speech going?' she asked.

'I'm still working on it.'

'You need only say a few words,' she said, trying to keep her tone light. 'Thank everyone for coming, remind them that the church needs a lot of work on the roof and that will cost a lot of money. Ask–'

'Ask them to enjoy themselves and spend generously,' Richard broke in testily. 'If that was all that was required, the vicar could have done the job himself.'

Ruth sighed softly. It looked as if they were in for Richard's 'State of the Nation' address. With a nod to her he returned to his study.

At half-past twelve, they had a glass of sherry together in the sitting room and then a light lunch of ham and salad, cheese and biscuits. She was relieved that Richard had already changed. It would mean that when she had tidied away the lunch things, she would have the upper floor to herself for half an hour.

When she reached her bedroom, she went to the wardrobe and taking out a silk dress, held it against her and looked at herself in the long mirror. Was the fuchsia pink too startling? After all, she would be standing beside Richard at the opening. Surely she was expected to put on a bit of a show? She laid the dress and the straw hat on the bed and went to the dressing table. Sliding open the drawer, she felt her way through the clutter of small articles until she found the package. As she anticipated, it bore a Madrid postmark. Now that she had it in her hand, she hesitated, delaying opening it while she ran her fingers over it trying to guess at the identity of the object inside.

In Madrid, she and Richard had lived in an airy apartment in what had once been a rather grand private house. It looked onto a broad, tree-lined avenue and was within a short walking distance of the British Embassy. It was a period of increasing tension between the Spanish Government and ETA, the separatist group that for years had been struggling to achieve autonomy for the Basque region in the north-west of the country.

Shortly after Richard had taken up his new posting, an ETA unit operating in Madrid had kidnapped Ramón Férez, a senior civil servant with the Ministry of the Interior. His driver and bodyguard had both been killed. Férez was in his early forties, married and had two children. Ironically, no one had tried harder than he to effect a rapprochement between the government and the separatists.

ETA issued an ultimatum. The government had seven days to agree to their demands or Férez would be executed. The government took a strong line. There would be no negotiations with terrorists. An anxious public was assured that no efforts would be spared to bring to justice those responsible for the outrage and to release the hostage.

Thousands of extra police were drafted in to the city, roadblocks set up, drivers stopped and questioned, vehicles searched. Apartments known to house those sympathetic to ETA were raided. Not a trace of the kidnappers or their victim was found and time was running out. The police came in for strong criticism. Many doubted whether they genuinely wanted the criminals caught and tried. Cynics took the view that the operation was largely a public-relations exercise. These misgivings were hardly allayed when the government held a reception for the press corps to which selected diplomats and their wives were invited.

'Preparing the ground for failure,' Richard said as they drove there. Férez would die. The government was concerned only with demonstrating that it had done what it could to save him.

'But, Richard, there has to be some middle way. A man's life is at stake.'

'There is no middle way, Ruth. I know it is distressing but that is the truth. If the government shows weakness now, it will be open season for hostage-taking. It won't be a case of one man's death, however deplorable that is – there could be dozens. So whatever private views you hold, keep them to yourself. Remember, you are not here as a private individual but as the wife of a senior–'

'*Oh, Richard, do stop pontificating!* This isn't the time for it.'

It was the second half of May and a warm evening. They were shown into a large, ornate room hung with gilt-framed mirrors and portraits of soldiers and statesmen. Tall windows with heavy crimson curtains gave on to an interior garden. The room was crowded, the conversation animated. Everyone seemed to have a smile on their face and a glass of wine in their hand. It might have been an interval between acts at the opera. It was difficult to believe that somewhere, perhaps not far from where she was standing, a man was lying in some dank, dark hole of a prison, chained like a dog and with only his fear and the smell of stale sweat for company.

Richard lengthened his stride, cutting off the escape route of a junior minister that he had hoped to talk to. He would be in a high good humour at dinner that evening. 'Effective diplomacy, Ruth, is all about giving the policy-makers a gentle nudge at the critical moment. I flatter myself that I have a finely attuned sense of timing.'

Making an excuse about going in search of a soft drink, she was moving to the edge of the room when she felt a tap on her arm. *'Alan!'* she gasped. *'You startled me!* What on earth are you doing in Madrid?'

'My paper sent me to cover this wretched Férez business. I thought I might find you here this evening.'

'If I could leave now, I would. Anything rather than be a part of this charade. How long have you been here?'

'I arrived yesterday.' His dark eyes held hers. 'I want to see you, talk to you. I promise not to make things difficult'

'I don't think we should meet. You have a job to do here. I'm sure Richard can–'

'It isn't Richard I want to see. It's you.'

'What about?' she breathed, suspicion flaring within her.

'I can't tell you now but it's important. It must be tomorrow. I wouldn't ask you to come to my hotel but–'

'*Your hotel!*' she hissed at him. 'Are you out of your mind? Anywhere but–'

'Anywhere but that?' He was amused. 'If you could see the hotel–'

'I don't want to see your hotel.' His smile infuriated her.

He shook his head in genuine perplexity. 'I would suggest the park but everywhere I go in this place I am followed.'

'*Followed!* I don't believe it. You are fantasising!' Her hand flew to her mouth. '*No!* I take that back.' Alan didn't fantasise. 'If it must be your hotel...'

'It's rather seedy but at least no one knows I'm there. The proprietor doesn't seem to have heard of a register. No doubt if one wanted to rent a room by the hour, he would be happy to oblige.'

'Now you tell me.' She ventured a smile.

But his features had tightened again. 'What time do you normally go shopping?'

'Ten o'clock.'

'Then meet me at half past. Don't take a taxi. When you get to the Plaza Mayor, walk the rest of the way.' He gave her a card with the address of the hotel. 'There is a primitive street map on the back. Try to memorise it and then–'

'Burn it? Or chew it into tiny pieces and swallow it?' she suggested, widening her eyes at him.

'We can have a laugh about this when it's over – but not now. When you get to the hotel, just ask for room eleven.'

'Alan, please tell me what this is–'

'Tomorrow, Ruth. I promise.' He pressed her hand and then he was gone.

***

The following day Richard left for the Embassy just before eight. Breakfast had been a sombre meal. He had pointed to the headlines in the newspaper. *'ETA deadline expires at midnight tomorrow,'* she read. As if anyone needed reminding. He inquired how she was spending the morning. Shopping as usual she had told him and then she had a hair appointment. She disliked telling lies but the question had been the more unexpected because she was joining him for a formal lunch at the Embassy.

Consuelo, their daily woman, arrived at half-past nine. At ten, Ruth took a last look at her street map, collected her shopping basket and descended the wide stone stairway to the street. It was already hot, the sky cloudless.

She took a bus to the Plaza Mayor and then walked, zigzagging through the narrow streets of the old town until she found the little alley. In the warm air, sheets hung motionless from crude metal balconies. From a window high above her she could hear a baby crying. Twice she walked past the hotel without knowing it. There was neither a sign nor a street number. Then she spotted the faded lettering over the doorway and pushed through a beaded curtain to the interior.

In the room to her left, two men with their backs to her were standing drinking. She would never understand how it was possible to consume alcohol at that hour and accomplish anything during the rest of the day. As she passed them they stopped talking and she realised that they could see her reflection in the long mirror behind the bar.

The man behind the reception desk was wearing a grubby, collarless shirt from which a profusion of shiny black hairs sprouted at the open neck.

She asked for the room number in a governessy tone of voice as if she had come to collect a recalcitrant child for an outing.

'*El tercer piso,*' he muttered without raising his eyes from the newspaper.

The odour of cheap spirits followed her round the bend of the steep wooden stairs before it was overwhelmed by a powerful smell of drains. A pile of sheets in a dark corner encouraged the hope that the establishment made a distinction between what was dirty and what was not.

The third floor landing was unlit and the room took some moments to find. She knocked tentatively on the door. It opened quickly and closed behind her.

'Good of you to come, Ruth. Especially to a hovel like this.'

He kissed her on the cheek and followed her eyes as she took in the wash basin coming away from the wall, the dingy carpet, the scuffed wallpaper, the empty whisky bottle in the waste basket.

'Alan, do you really have to live in–'

'In a tip like this?' He went to the window and tugged at the skimpy curtains in a vain attempt to draw them together against the fierce sunlight. 'No, but there is an uncomfortable degree of interest in my movements. In a place like this, the hare can lose the hounds for a few hours.'

She fanned her cheeks with her hand. The room was very warm. 'If you were to open the curtains, you might encourage a little air in my direction.'

'I'm sorry, Ruth, but I think we should leave them drawn.' He stowed some papers into a grip and pulled up the zip.

'Are you on the move again?'

'Yes. I'm checking out as soon as you are safely on your way. I shall be in another hotel tonight.'

'Something a little more civilised, I hope.'

'I like my creature comforts as much as the next man provided that they don't get in the way of doing the job.' He drew up an upright chair for her and sat down on the edge of the sagging mattress.

'Were there two men in the bar when you came in?'

'Yes. Two workmen.'

He grimaced. 'Certainly they were dressed as workmen. But they got out of a shiny black saloon car a hundred yards down the road and walked here. It didn't add up.'

'Policemen?'

'Maybe.' He pulled at an ear lobe and frowned. 'Already I regret bringing you here.'

'But I want...' It was too late to snatch back the words. She avoided his eyes. 'I want to help if I can.'

'You are helping – just by being here.' He shook a cigarette into his hand. 'Does the name Xavier Zorilla mean anything to you?'

'Isn't he one of the top men in ETA?'

Alan released a small cloud of smoke at the ceiling. 'Zorilla is the head of the ETA unit that is holding Ramón Férez. The police probably suspect that I have made contact with him.'

'And have you?'

'Yes.'

'*But, Alan, that is madness!* Leave ETA to the police!'

Her voice had risen and he put a warning finger to his lips. 'Half the police in the country are meant to be looking for Férez but they haven't made a very good job of it so far.'

'Does your paper know what you are doing?'

'They know as much as they need to know.'

'How did you find Zorilla?'

'I got a lucky break. I knew very little about ETA. Only what I had picked up over the years or could dig out of the newspaper archives. I thought it would be easier here in Madrid but getting people to talk was like pulling teeth.'

'Are you surprised? People are too frightened! Did you try the Press Association?'

'Of course. It's good for a free drink but if you want to find out something you cannot read in *El Pais*, you have to do some burrowing.'

She pointed at his crumpled linen suit. 'So that explains it.'

He stubbed out his half-smoked cigarette. 'Sitting around in clubs and bars and cellars hasn't done it any favours.'

'Who did you talk to?'

He shrugged. 'You find them in every city. People who want to remake the world. Artists, writers, poets, dreamers, drunkards. All subversives in their own way. I found this odd little man, Rafael Colom. A straggly beard and a messianic light in his eye. Just skin and bone ... a dusty black suit falling off him...'

'How does a man like that live?'

'Colom runs an underground press out of a basement somewhere. He prints pamphlets, news-sheets. Far left stuff. Puts the boot into establishment figures, the church, the military, politicians. I have a smattering of the language and he could speak a sort of bastard English.'

'You must have made a great pair.'

Alan laughed. 'It was certainly a lively evening. We finished up in an all-night bar. Still arguing. I told him that ETA was just a bunch of gangsters. By that time I was tanked up on the local brandy. He took the bait. Read me the riot act. Warned me to choose my company more carefully if I was going to talk like that or I would be lucky to leave Spain in a wheelchair.'

'Alan, you are asking for trouble.'

'Ramón Férez has already got trouble. From what I have heard about him, he is worth a risk or two.'

'How can ETA murder a man like Férez? Doesn't public opinion mean anything to them? Even in the Basque region there have been huge protest demonstrations against them.'

'ETA do not want Férez's death. What they want is status. Recognition.'

'In order to make demands that no government could accept,' she replied hotly.

'Perhaps. But ETA argue that by refusing to negotiate, the government has turned them into outlaws.'

'So we have had murder and extortion for decades. Isn't it time they tried something else?'

'They are going to try something else,' he said quietly.

'Alan, what are you saying?'

'I pushed Colom very hard. Terrorism had failed. ETA should appeal over the heads of their government. Use the world press.'

'How did he react?'

'He laughed. *The capitalist press!* Why should they help? By that time the drink was doing the talking for me. I said that my paper would give ETA the centre pages so that they could put their case, and syndicate it worldwide in exchange for Ramón Férez's release.'

'You were bluffing. You couldn't bind your editor.'

'It was a hell of a gamble but I believed I could get the paper to back me. Colom reckoned that he could put together an article that ETA would approve and they might be persuaded to do a deal. I called him yesterday as I was instructed. Every hour on the hour. A few minutes after midday, Zorilla telephoned. I can't tell you what the arrangements are but it's all fixed up.'

'Has your editor given you the go-ahead?'

'I called him late last night. I was running out of time or I wouldn't have called him from here.'

'Was that a mistake? That man downstairs in reception. Do you think he was listening in?'

'Possibly. I had to chance it.'

'Was your editor prepared to back you?'

'If ETA release Férez into the hands of the International Red Cross, the paper will print that article. He will have to run it past the lawyers first but he won't make unnecessary changes.'

'And if something goes wrong?'

'I am on my own.'

'And the police?' Ruth stood up and went to the window.

'They are to be kept out of it.'

'*Alan, it's crazy!* You don't know this country. Or its people. What makes you think you can trust a man like Zorilla? How can you be sure that Férez is still alive?'

Alan put his arms around her, held her to him. 'The only thing that is crazy is to be here with you and talking about those hoodlums.'

She struggled in his arms. 'Let me go, Alan. *It's not fair!*'

'If we love each other...'

She broke free. 'How can we love each other? Love is more than spending a few hours together. Richard and I ...' she began, 'what we have may not be very special but I am all he has got.'

'You loved me then. You cannot have forgotten.'

She turned to him and took his hands. 'Alan, you were ill. You needed to shut out the world for a few days. I just happened to be there to hold the door closed.' To her astonishment she found she was weeping.

'And now?'

'Now ...' she dabbed at her eyes, 'now you seem to have gone completely mad.'

'It's a mad world.'

She shook her head. 'You wouldn't do this if you meant what you said a moment ago.'

Very gently, with the tips of his fingers he brushed the tears from her cheeks. 'Do you remember what you said to me once? You said that the world couldn't afford lookers-on. That things had got beyond that point. That we have to intervene ... however inadequately ... we have to make a stand.'

'I didn't mean that you have to–'

'Yes, you did. And now you must be on your way.'

***

Her fingers closed around the contents of the package. When she had given the policeman her address, she had the feeling that he would write to her. But after all this time what difference did it make? Why revive those memories? Accusation. Counter-accusation. ETA denouncing Alan as a police stooge. The police insisting that Alan had acted alone, that he was blind to everything but the chance of the scoop of a lifetime.

The note was wrapped around a small audio tape identical in appearance to those that she used to type Richard's letters. The dictation machine was on a table next to her writing desk. Was Richard still safely downstairs? She opened her bedroom door quietly but her husband must have heard her for he called up to her, 'Ruth, I am just going to run through my notes with the vicar. I thought we should stand on the terrace this year. My voice will carry better from the top of the steps.'

'You will have the microphone, Richard.'

'Nevertheless ...' he recovered himself after this small check, 'I think that is the place to be, with the vicar on my left and you on my right.'

She closed her eyes. 'That seems sensible.'

'Yes, but on reflection, perhaps the relative positions should be reversed.'

'If you feel strongly about it...'

'I feel that–'

'Do whatever you think best, Richard. I'm in the middle of changing.'

'Very well. But I want you down in twenty minutes. Half-past two. *On the dot!*' A few moments later she heard his brisk, nervous step under her window.

The note was in Spanish, handwritten and unsigned. *'This tape,'* it read, *'is police property. The voice that you hear is that of Commissario General Juan Blastro, head of our Anti-Terrorist Unit at the time of Señor Dacre's death. Blastro was killed in a car explosion a month later. I had the task of clearing out his office and found the tape in his safe. Had I given it to my superior officers at the time, they would have destroyed it. You must judge whether I did right. I rely on you to destroy both this note and the recording. Whatever you decide, I send you my good wishes for the future.'*

Ruth switched on the machine and inserted the tape. She did not start the playback but took a chair and read the last sentence slowly once more. *'Whatever you decide.'* It was oddly phrased.

Three weeks earlier, on the twentieth of May, the last day of her stay with her sister, she had gone to the cemetery. As usual, Debbie offered to drive her. As usual, she thanked her but no, she would take the bus and then walk the last half mile. Debbie gave her a long look and an enigmatic kiss on the cheek.

It was a hot afternoon. The heat seemed to have leached all the colour from the sky. The cemetery was on the edge of the city surrounded by a high wall. Inside everything seemed dry and parched, the paths dusty, the grass already burnt. There was a troubling wind and she was glad of the cotton scarf about her head.

Alan's grave was in the shadow of a tall cypress. That was why she hadn't seen the man at once, why she had been so startled and upset. She wanted to be alone. Alone with Alan. Just the two of them for a few minutes in the year. Was it so much to ask?

As he straightened, she saw that he was in police uniform. He was stockily built with black hair combed straight back from his forehead. He had only to turn and go but he stood his ground, looking at her with curiosity.

She found herself trembling with anger. What was this unbeliever doing here of all places? *Today of all days*. Had he known Alan Dacre, she asked him, struggling to keep her voice under control? No? Then what was he doing there?

'Is it customary in your country to ask policemen to account for their presence in a public cemetery?' He was unsmiling, his tone gently ironic.

'My husband was First Secretary at the British Embassy here when ... when Mr Dacre was killed.'

'Your husband? The First Secretary, you say?' He floundered for a moment. 'But that was many years ago.'

'My husband arranged for Mr Dacre to be buried here.' Why did she have to explain anything? Or defend herself to this man?

'Señor Dacre left instructions with you, I believe. Not your husband.'

'Perhaps. I cannot remember. It was long ago. It is not important any more.'

'Maybe. But it was unusual that his body was not sent home.'

'Señor Dacre – Alan – had no real family, no home. At any rate, nowhere he thought of as home. But even if he had, I think he would have wanted to remain here.' She had thrown a scrap to this importunate creature. Now, perhaps, he would leave her in peace.

'I hoped that you would say that.'

'He had given this country everything else.' Her voice was harsh with strain.

'Do you not think that Señor Dacre would only claim for himself that he had tried to save the life of one man?'

'Let's be generous, shall we?' she flashed back at him, anger and misery curdling inside her. 'Let us give him the benefit of the doubt. Today of all days.'

The policeman bent down and straightened the vase at the base of the headstone. 'Were you in love with Alan Dacre?'

This was persecution. She took a deep breath and loosened the knot under her chin, removed the scarf and shook out her hair. 'Isn't that my business?'

'We all have secrets. It helps sometimes if we can share them.'

'You must speak for yourself.'

'I do speak for myself.'

She wrapped her arms tight about herself. 'What use are we to him now? Our prayers are too late.'

'Our prayers are for ourselves,' the policeman replied quietly. 'We come here to honour him. You in your way; I in mine.'

She crouched down at the foot of the headstone to hide her face. Adding her flowers to his, mingling them inexpertly, the tears falling on her hands. 'Not an hour goes by when I do not think of him. Not a day passes when I do not pray to him to let me go. To let me forget him.'

'Do you have children?'

'We had a son. He died.'

'I'm truly very sorry.' He placed a hand under her elbow and helped her to her feet. 'I wonder what sort of a life you live in England?'

'An ordinary sort of life.'

'You look after your husband and the house. You do the shopping. Perhaps, at the weekend, you go to neighbours for a game of bridge. You take occasional holidays. Once a year you come to Spain by yourself.'

'Something like that.' This relentless probing. How strange that she did not resent it.

'Is that enough for a woman like you?'

'There is nothing very special about me.'

'I believe you were doing relief work in Africa when you met?'

She shrugged. 'I was one of a team. That's all.'

He seemed reluctant to go. She had the impression that he wanted to say more, that their discussion was incomplete in some way. When she got back to England, it still gnawed away at her. She had immersed herself in a round of charitable activities, even joined a bridge club, but it hadn't made any difference. Her heart still skipped a beat when the mail clattered into the letter box.

She undressed to her slip and, going to the bathroom, washed her hands. Then returning to her bedroom, she pressed the button of the dictation machine. Walking quickly to the dressing table, she sat in front of the mirror.

The machine crackled into life. 'Juan Blastro speaking. I am sorry to put you to so much trouble but I thought it best that you did not call from the Embassy.'

'It is most inconvenient, Commissario General. I have a busy morning. It has meant rearranging an appointment. I am hosting an important luncheon at one.'

It was Richard's voice. Shockingly unexpected and yet, somehow, inevitable. She ran to the door and stood with her back against it, her hands flat against the wood panels, her lips pressed together to still the sound of her breathing.

'We are both busy men, Señor Gage, and have no time to waste so I shall come straight to the point. Does the name Alan Dacre mean anything to you?'

'The newspaper chap? I have met him but not since I took up my appointment here. Why do you ask?'

'Your wife and he are friends?'

'Acquaintances. I would put it no higher. But what has this to do with–'

'Señor Gage, Alan Dacre has been in Spain for three days. For the past twenty-four hours he has been under police surveillance. Your wife was seen speaking to him at the press reception yesterday.'

'And why should they not meet? I imagine it was merely–'

'Please allow me to finish. Your wife was also seen going into Dacre's hotel at half-past ten this morning.'

'You must be mistaken. Ruth and I had breakfast together. She was going shopping and then she had to go to her hairdresser. She is joining me for lunch.'

'The report is reliable, I assure you. On my desk I have a photograph taken from a house across the street from the hotel where Dacre spent last night. It shows your wife and Dacre together in the bedroom.'

'No doubt there is a perfectly innocent explanation. General Blastro, you cannot have forgotten that today is the twentieth of May and, according to my watch, a few minutes short of noon. ETA's ultimatum expires at midnight. Ramón Férez has a fraction over twelve hours to live. Have your men nothing better to do with their time than follow women about the streets?'

'My department believes that Dacre is in contact with the head of the ETA unit that is holding Férez.'

'That is incredible!'

'On the contrary. A prestigious English newspaper has resources that we lack. My information is that a meeting between Zorilla and Dacre has been set up for three o'clock this afternoon. We want to know what your wife was doing in that hotel. Was she helping Dacre in his negotiations with a terrorist organisation or was her visit ... a social one?'

'I dislike your tone, Blastro. May I remind you that I am a senior diplomat at the British Embassy? Have a care or I shall report this.'

'You would do better to consider your own position, Señor Gage. By tomorrow Dacre may be a national figure. He is certainly a colourful one. Secret meetings with ETA. Assignations with the wife of a British diplomat in a squalid backstreet hotel. Can you imagine what the press will make of it?'

'Your insinuations are disgusting.'

'I am asking for the facts, Señor Gage. Insinuations are for others.'

There was a long pause before Richard spoke again. 'I want that photograph back,' he said at last.

'Help us to give Dacre some protection and you shall have it back.'

'Are the police really interested in protecting him?'

'Of course. He may be a reckless fool but we don't want his death on our conscience.'

A long sigh. 'What do you want me to do?'

'We want you to delay him at his hotel for a few moments. That is all.'

'It is most inconvenient. We have important guests. What is the point of it?'

'That is our affair.'

'Where is he staying?'

'At the Hotel Irun. Behind it there is a large underground car park. ETA will park one of their cars there at exactly one o'clock this afternoon. Under the passenger floor mat, Dacre will find the keys and instructions telling him how to get to the rendezvous.'

'How do you know all this?'

'We have our contacts.'

'How do I explain how I knew where to find him?'

'Tell him you contacted his paper. You were concerned for his safety. You had to know where he was staying.'

'Supposing his paper doesn't know it?'

'They do know it. Dacre is waiting for a call from his editor.'

'I congratulate you on your spy system.'

'It is my job to know what is happening. What time do you have on your watch?'

'Six minutes past twelve.'

'Good. Be at the Hotel Irun in half an hour. Now, this is very important. Keep Dacre talking until five minutes past the hour. Ten minutes would be better still.'

'While you tamper with his car?'

'You ask too many questions.'

'ETA will be watching.'

'Not there, they won't. My men will see to that.'

'Then they will be across the road. Above a shop, perhaps, or in a telephone kiosk. If Dacre doesn't drive out of that car park within moments of that car being delivered or if any of your men is spotted, it is as good as a death sentence.'

'We know our business. Just worry about yourself.'

'How can I delay him? Why should he listen to me?'

'Use your authority. Dacre is a citizen of the United Kingdom. Warn him that his activities have come to the attention of the authorities, that what he is doing is not only dangerous but illegal.'

'I have no authority. You are the policeman. If you know where Dacre is, why don't you arrest him?'

'Because I dare not. His newspaper will claim that he has done a deal with ETA. That Férez was on the point of being released when we intervened. It would do us enormous damage.'

'Don't you want to see Ramón Férez released?'

'Of course. But if ETA is to be rewarded for years of kidnapping, murder and extortion by a whitewashing from the world's press, Spain is paying a very high price. Excuse me, I must take this call...'

Ruth went to the window. People were drifting past the trestle tables. Some were already gathering on the lawn in front of the steps. Richard was in earnest conversation with the vicar and the treasurer of the parish council.

Blastro's voice again, 'That was the International Red Cross. They have received a coded message from ETA asking them to keep a line open until an hour after midnight.'

'So?'

'So ETA expect to get what they want from Dacre. They are making preparations to release Férez.'

'That photograph–'

'One thing at a time, Señor Gage. Keep Dacre talking until five minutes past one o'clock. Then you will get your photograph.' The line went dead.

Ruth switched off the machine. She put on her clothes quickly, found her shoes and her hat and stood in front of the long mirror, adjusting the brim mechanically, as if she was dressing a model in a shop window.

***

A little after two o'clock that afternoon, driving through open country north of the city, Alan had been killed by a bomb in a culvert detonated by command wire. ETA had claimed responsibility. The English reporter, they insisted, was a police spy. There had been speculation that some sort of tracking device had been fitted to the vehicle. The police denied any involvement. Dacre, they said, had only himself to blame. By acting on his own he had made their task impossible and his failure to do a deal with ETA had made Ramón Férez's death inevitable.

Richard had telephoned her at the Embassy to say that he would be late. She was to make his apologies to their guests. He joined them at half-past one. At lunch, she had caught his eyes on her. There was something in them that she couldn't read. He drank too much and talked over-loudly. It was out of key with the mood of his guests. The knowledge of ETA's ultimatum hung heavily over their spirits.

***

She glanced at her watch. *Heavens!* She was nearly ten minutes late. She hurried down the stairs and almost collided with her husband in the hall. *'Good God, woman!'* he shouted, working himself into a passion. 'What *have* you been doing? *We are all waiting for you!* I told you to be on time. Does the concept of a deadline hold *any* meaning for you?'

She often reflected in later years that if he had said anything else at that moment, anything at all, she would probably have stayed with him.

In Brief

Charles Owen writes the Army obituaries for the Daily Telegraph. He has been variously a stockbroker, a merchant banker, a cavalry officer, a Ministry of Defence contractor and an engineering export salesman. *Cry Cassandra!* and *Fiamma* were published recently. Four collections of short stories – *A Crack in the Glass, The Mark of the Beast, Man Overboard* and *Escapade* – are now being published simultaneously.

Meet the Author, Charles Owen

I was born in 1935. When the Second World War broke out a few years later, I was shipped off from a Devonshire hill farm to Australia. My father, who was wounded in the First World War, was then in MI5. He believed that the Germans might invade and probably wanted my mother, sister and myself out of the way.

In 1942, we were returning to England when we were torpedoed by a German submarine in the North Atlantic. The ship was sent to the bottom but after taking to the waves in a lifeboat we were all rescued by the US Navy.

Aged 12, I went to Eton. Top hats were being phased out. They were routinely maltreated until the boys wearing them looked like something out of the music hall. But if the school was slowly changing, the house where I boarded lacked all mod cons and was later pulled down.

In 1956, in my first term at Cambridge and despite the objections of the Foreign Office, I set off to Budapest in the hope of helping the Hungarians in their revolution against the Soviets. My involvement made little difference to the outcome of that tragic affair but the experience provided the inspiration for my forthcoming book, *The Dido Decrypt*.

I did my National Service with a cavalry regiment in Germany. Our job was to discourage the Red Army from crossing the Rhine. As a tank commander, it was wise to keep well in with your driver. If he was cross with you, he would give you a bumpy ride which would loosen every tooth in your head.

A spell in stock-broking and merchant banking persuaded me that I was better at making things than making money and there followed many productive years as the export director of an engineering company. We were contractors to the Ministry of Defence and there was a lot of travelling to the Middle East. The work was absorbing, exacting and, sometimes, frightening.

In 2000, for the Daily Telegraph, I began writing up the stories of the surviving men and women who had been awarded the Victoria Cross or the George Cross. That led to writing the obituaries of those who had had adventurous and distinguished careers in the British Army. To date, several hundred of these can be read on the internet.

In the course of reading private papers and unpublished memoirs that have passed through my hands, I became fascinated by the exciting and often perilous careers of servicemen and women who were involved in Intelligence operations; spies and counter-spies, secret agents and members of the Special Operations Executive who were parachuted into enemy-occupied countries to train and arm the Resistance. *The Voce Vendetta*, relating the fictional exploits of Captain Rohan Voce, will be published in 2016 and will, I hope, bring an account of some of these clandestine operations to a wider readership.

Acknowledgements

My heartfelt thanks go to Georgie, my daughter, who helped to unravel the seemingly impenetrable mysteries of the word processor, also to my son, Jamie, whose guidance has proved invaluable in my wanderings through the trackless wastes of journalism; and to Pierre, my brother-in-law, whose expertise, unstintingly shared, kept my spirits up and my blood pressure down when the hardware and software sulked or threatened to mutiny. I have nothing but praise for the unwinking editorial eyes of the proof-readers. Rosie, heroically volunteered to give the manuscript a final vetting. Any errors that remain are my responsibility.